CANINE EFFECTS ON THE PRICE OF WATER

AND OTHER SHORT STORIES

CLIFF WILLIAMSON

Photography by
CLIFF WILLIAMSON

The stories contained in this book are works of fiction. Names, characters, businesses, places, events, locales, and incidents are either the products of the author's imagination or used in a fictitious manner. Any resemblance to actual persons, living or dead, or actual events is purely coincidental.

Copyright © 2021 Cliff Williamson

All rights reserved.

CONTENTS

"In The Lion's Den"	1
Canine Effects on the Price of Water	16
Time Bomb	22
Heart 4.0	33
Live by the Sword	45
"TAILS"	59
Man Overboard	63
EIGHT	66
How Was Your Day?	83
End of Violence	88
Acknowledgments	105
About the Author	107

FOREWORD

Fall, Fontana Lake, North Carolina

Hello, and welcome to my collection of short stories, written over a period of 20 years.

The oldest are the selections from my novel, *Shining New Testament*. *"Tails"* is a description of a futuristic fashion show featuring genetic manipulations rather than clothing. *"In The Lion's Den"* is a chapter of a section of the book written by the Gospel Jane. (Yes, in my New Testament the gospels are Matias, Marcos, Luigi, and Jane.) All the rest stand alone and have been inspired by events, places I have lived, and the people I have met.

I have lived in Argentina for more than half of my life, residing in Buenos Aires, a lovely and artistically stimulating city of 16 million inhabitants. This is the home of one of the world's greatest writers Jose Luis Borges and other fine writers such as Julio Cortázar. There are enough theatres in the city so that you could attend a new one every night for two years without repeating. The rest of the country is filled with beauty. *Canine Effects on the Price of Water* was inspired by the beautiful and remote landscapes of Patagonia. *End of Violence* takes place in Cordoba, which truly is the peanut capital of Argentina and a place of violent storms.

    A few stories are just plain crazy fun, like *EIGHT*, the story of the precocious octopus, and *HEART 4.0*, about a robot who finds love in the time of climate change.

    Live by the Sword and *Time Bomb* tell how violence and powerful weapons ultimately affect the lives of those who practice the dark arts, as well as the people who associate with them.

    Man Overboard is a short little horror story, and *How Was Your Day?* is a dreamlike experience that happened to me and my wife while on holiday in Western North Carolina.

    Please enjoy. Read and share, and hopefully, read again!

Cliff Williamson, August 2020

"IN THE LION'S DEN"
FROM SHINING NEW TESTAMENT, BOOK OF JANE, CHAPTER 3

My life was a dream until I turned eleven, each day sweet as a Cadbury chocolate, melting in my mouth at night as I went to sleep, replenished the next day by another even sweeter. It was the best life I ever knew. Too bad it came all at once, at the beginning. I could use some of that sweetness now.

I was the second child of Jon and Greta Vandenberg, white South Africans who moved to Zimbabwe to homestead. We settled in *Chinhoyi*. Father bought land and built up our farm outside Lion's Den, a little village near a stand of grain silos. He raised maize, tobacco, cattle, and cotton. It was a proud place, a showpiece of order and efficiency, and my parents were admired as honest, fair-minded folk.

My older sister and I were raised under blue skies on the fertile veldt. Herds of twitching impala and kudu were the backdrop to our childhood. With my mother we watched a *vervet* give birth to spindly babies. We threw fruit at the *bo'bos* in *Maponi* trees and laughingly dodged their return fire. We slept each night feeling loved and safe, assuming it would last forever.

Father could have been anything, but farmer and rancher was the life he chose. His wife of five years came with him from an ever more dangerous Johannesburg, together with daughter Maggie, age four, and me one month in the womb. Zimbabwe was perfect. *Chinhoyi* had all that my parents wanted.

Money was never a problem. We didn't think of ourselves as elite, though undoubtedly we were. We were happy to share our good fortune. Father respected everyone. He hired teachers for the children of the workers and was generous on holidays, birthdays, and festivals. Mother's three maids, cook, and houseboy loved her dearly and worshipped her for the opportunities she provided them.

But all was not well in Zimbabwe.

Violence against whites intensified during the late 1990s. President Mugabe got himself into an electoral bind and knew he would lose the next election if he didn't take desperate action to win votes. His solution was to attack the white farmers, the large landholders with visible wealth. Rape and murder became commonplace. Waves of viciousness crept ever closer to our home, spreading like strep in a Petri dish.

Mugabe encouraged persecution of the whites, claiming our wealth was ill-gotten on the backs of the poor. The government targeted farms for acquisition and instigated compulsory land sales. But many who identified themselves as "war veterans" couldn't wait their turn, and came to squat on the verandas of country estates. They demanded food and drinks. They insisted on apologies for the theft of the land. Once a neighbour's farm was invaded, your farm would likely be next.

Father did what he could to ensure protection for the local landowners. He played golf with the high officials at the local club in Lion's Den, attempting to make friends with the district police commission. Together they put down many *Lions* – the local beer – as Father stretched time before the inevitable occurred.

When it came, the world paid little heed. White persecution was a battle cry rarely heard and hard to fathom. We faced an onslaught of injustice with varying degrees of courage, fear, and finally surrender.

First, our neighbour's farm to the south was occupied for three weeks by veterans who sat in the comfortable chairs on the veranda surrounding the house. They insisted on their right to the land, menacing until our neighbours finally gave up and left.

To the north, our neighbours held out longer. They withdrew behind the high fences around the house and main barns. But their horse stable lay outside the gates, and the invaders stacked hay around the horses, soaked the bales with gasoline, and burned twelve mares to death, animals which my sister and I rode often during our school holidays.

In the summer of 2002 when I turned eleven, our parents sat us down at the supper table. Mum was going to London to look for a new home, and within six months we would move away, probably forever. I cried like I'd been beaten. Father held me by the shoulders, smiled, and winked at me, and I trusted we'd be ok. He could always make me feel safe and loved. He was the best.

Mum wanted to take us with her but relented for practical reasons. She could search more freely without the burden of caring for us. Father felt we needed time to bid goodbye to the land, and I think he wanted us with him for those final days in paradise.

We drove Mother to *Harare* for a flight to Johannesburg, and from there to London. She sent cheerful postcards every day describing the city, the large well-organized schools, girls in uniform, the tube, the historical buildings, and the foods of all ethnic varieties. She painted a lovely picture for us, but I was sure I would not fit within its frame. "What are the monkeys like?" I wanted to ask. "Are there antelope to hunt? Is there drumming to announce the harvest fest? Where will a girl like me fit in?"

Maggie was more settled to the idea, as she had reached her womanhood and the prospects in Zimbabwe for a despised minority were not enticing. Her boyfriend Zachary would be off to London soon and their relationship could continue unabated. But understanding how a boy could be more interesting than a monkey was still a few years outside my purview, and Maggie's incessant primping in the mirror disgusted me.

Zach had the full approval of my parents. Mum loved to feed him, and he often hunted for meat with Father. One time they tracked a leopard which was taking our calves two a week. A neighbour finally shot it, but a strong bond developed between my father and Zach during those days. Zach's mum was very ill, and his father took up drink. Zach was welcomed like a son in our house, and Father said he was an excellent shot.

One afternoon Father was reinforcing security on the perimeter fence. I was in my room working on maths after a brief snack of meat pies and *Mazoe Orange Crush*, which I loved, always served ice cold. We were required to study or read whether we had homework or not. Maggie was in her room, books open at her desk, ready to rush to feign study should the screen door slam signalling Father's return to the house. I knew she was admiring herself, exposing her blossoming profile to various angles in the mirror. I rolled my eyes every time I saw or even thought of it.

The farmhands were in the fields working the ground for planting. Father would have been there too, except that Mum had urged him to concentrate on security, and leave us girls alone as little as possible. Fibian the houseboy assisted Father, hammering in the added supports on the twelve-foot fence which surrounded the house and barns. Father wanted a stronger gate and set himself to reinforcing it with metal posts. Two maids were napping in their rooms, soon to rise and prepare our dinner. The cook had her day off, and a third maid was calling on her sick mum in *Mbare* – a crowded township outside *Harare*. The house was quiet, except for the distant sound of hammers, and Father's casual exchange of friendly insults with Fibian. Their specialty was besting the other with fictional comparisons to animals, exaggerating their inadequacies.

"You hammer like a woodpecker with a broken beak!" Father said.

"And you, sir! You hold that post like an old lady elephant with the palsy!" Fibian replied. They chuckled and continued their work.

I was daydreaming of Mum, and at the same time thinking that when I finished my last problem I'd make sandwiches to take out to Father and Fibian. There was Black Cat Peanut Butter in the green bottle on the pantry shelf. I could help too. I could hammer as well as any of the workmen, perhaps not as good as Father, but good enough. He told me that a woman could do anything a man could do except piddle standing up. Mum said I could do that too if there was good reason, but she made clear she was not recommending it. If only I could finish this last problem, I could get out there and do something before the dinner call.

"If a train left *Harare* station heading for *Mutare* at 2:00 PM, and travelled 100 km per hour…"

"Ha!" I laughed. Clearly the author of this book had never ridden a train in Zimbabwe. The engine would explode like a bomb if pushed to such a speed, and the cars would rattle to pieces.

"…and another train left *Mutare* for *Harare* …" Again unlikely. Few trains were running anymore, and certainly, the train that went would be the same one returning, with luck the next day after massive repairs, if the engineers were not striking, if the steel rails had not been stolen to be sold for scrap. This was a complete fairy tale.

I heard a truck coming up the long drive, maybe the returning workers, although it seemed early for that. Perhaps a piece of machinery had broken down and the men came home to tell Father. Or a neighbour needed to borrow a post-hole digger. Neighbours were forever borrowing Father's post-hole digger. He loaned his tools out freely, even though they didn't always come back.

Moments later, I heard the screen door creak open and Father yelled up the stairs, more loudly than necessary. "Girls, stay inside. Lock the doors. Don't' come out 'til I call you."

I wanted to rush to Maggie's room and catch her springing to her desk to pretend to study, but then reconsidered the tone of Father's voice. I ran downstairs. He stood at the door holding his rifle. I could see his pearl-handled Lugar sticking up from his belt. I opened my mouth to speak, but he shushed me with his finger.

"Do as I say. I'll be there just now." He walked out and let the door slam. Mum said slamming doors drove her crazy.

I ran to the window at the end of the hallway. Father made long strides back to the gate, covering the distance in no time.

Fibian was standing just inside the gate. A gravel truck was idling outside with a driver leaning awkwardly on the open door, head poking through the window, his leg out but not touching the ground. Five men stood in the truck bed, gawking over the cab. Two of them wore sunglasses, which I thought strange. Workmen don't wear sunglasses. They wear caps.

Fibian was protesting, flailing his arms as he did when he was excited, which was most of the time, saying the load of gravel must be for someone further up the road. Fibian spoke *Shona*, which I understood perfectly, but the driver must have been from beyond the Big Valley and spoke an unfamiliar dialect. I didn't like the way he half sat - half stood, leaning out of the door like he was preparing to run. I felt sick in my belly.

Maggie joined me at the window and took in the situation with her eyes. "What did Father say?"

"He said lock the doors." I watched the action at the gate. Father pointed the rifle barrel at the dusty ground. Despite his soothing tones, the driver grew more animated, indicating father's gun, trying to shame him for even showing a weapon when friendly strangers approached. I could hear him repeating the word 'veteran.'

The window in the hallway was painted shut, so I heard only

bits of conversation. The gestures said enough. The driver stepped from truck and approached the gate, shaking his head and waving his arms as Fibian did, as if to say that it was an insult to him and to his people to be greeted in such a manner in their own land, that Father and Fibian should be ashamed for suspecting folks trying to do their job.

Though I believed Maggie was forever lost to the silliness of adulthood, she grasped the danger more quickly than me.

"Jane, lock the doors," she said. "Get down the guns. Wake the maids. Then meet me upstairs."

That was much to remember. I stood rerunning her instructions through my head as she ran to the phone at the top of the stairs.

'Hello, please listen!' I heard her say, but I knew I had to move too. I heard nothing more of her call.

The next time I saw her, Maggie was changed forever.

I slid the heavy bolt into the hasp on the front door. I raced for the back door behind the kitchen, but stopped to peer out a small window when I heard a pop like the clapping of hands in Amory Cavern. My view was obstructed, but I heard Fibian scream like a woman. Bevelled glass blurred my view too much to make sense of it. I couldn't decide whether to lock the back door as Father said or to rush to the bay window in the alcove where I could see what happened to Fibian. I heard Maggie shouting "Jane, hurry!"

I ran to the back door and locked it, then raced back to the alcove. This window was large and exposed, and I felt unprotected standing there. Father planned to bar the windows of the house, but that would not happen today.

Fibian lay face down in the dust. Father was on one knee, his rifle pointing up from a prone position, the best for firing a gun. He shot twice and I saw a man on the truck bed fly backwards into the dump box. His mates ducked behind the cab.

The driver stepped out from behind the truck, reaching around the fender with an old revolver in his hand. He pointed without looking, firing wildly at Father, who turned to him to return fire but not before taking a bullet to his neck.

I saw a gush of red, enough that he would surely come in for bandages if this had been an accident. But it wasn't over yet. Father rocked back on his side, firing again over his legs at the crouching driver. This was not the best way to fire a gun. Still, the driver retreated behind the fat tire of his vehicle and shrieked to the men still in the truck bed, loud, so I heard it plainly.

"Kill the white bastard. If you cowards want shares you can't hide all day. Shoot him!"

Father was down, propping himself on his elbow, blood soaking the collar of his shirt. I screamed to him but I'm not sure he heard me through the unopened window. He glanced slowly back at the house. He'd want me to get the guns. I knew that much.

I ran to the pantry where the guns were stored, high on the shelves of canned pickles and beets and tomatoes. These were the guns not often used, though I fired them before. Maggie had too. Neither of us were good marksmen, but we knew how to load, aim, and pull a trigger, and how to hold tight so as not to feel the kick. I could hit a Lion's Beer can in the front yard if Maggie didn't make me giggle.

I stood on the stool, heard more shooting, and saw Agnes our cook pushing her heavy bulk past the pantry door from her room in the back of the kitchen. "What the devil is dis noise? G'wine to wake the dead," she said.

I sat on the floor in the pantry, two guns across my lap, boxes of cartridges spilled out in front of me. I sobbed something about Father's neck as I fought bullets into the stiff old Mouser Aught-6 first, then shells into the 12-gauge. I heard the whining motor of the truck coming closer, low gear and high RPM, much too loud. I screamed out, "Maggie!" and then, WHAM!

I fell onto my side, both loaded guns clattering off my lap onto the floor. With the sound of crumbling stone and plaster, two jars of beetroot exploded at my feet, splashing juice and round red slices across the linoleum. Impossibly, the truck engine sounds were coming from the living room. I stood, picked up the shotgun, and stumbled out to investigate.

I peered across the entryway, my back to the kitchen. The rear of the truck was *inside* the living room. Daylight showed over the top of its short tailgate. The veterans had bashed the truck into the corner of the house, breaking down a section of adjoining walls and part of the ceiling. The rug from mother's sewing room hung down like a banner through a hole in the ceiling. Four big tires sat two on a side atop the cream coloured carpet, a sofa crushed beneath the rear axle.

Daisy the maid ran past me and out the back door. Seconds later, I heard a shot.

Maggie screamed from upstairs, "Run Jane, Run!" like she was crying out from a primary reader at school.

But it was all too much. "Where can I run?" I wondered. "Run Jane, but where? Run and hide? Run and get help? Run to Father?"

The fat cook backed around the corner from the kitchen, her big bottom blocking my view, squeezing me back into the pantry like a tanker. Without looking back she beckoned to me with her hand and her voice.

"Come close, missy" she whispered. "Come, child, stay with Aggie now. Hold my hand, baby. Can you shoot that thing? Oh, lord, protect your servant Agnes and these little ones," she prayed. "See us through, oh lord…"

A sinister face with yellowed teeth came into view, raised a pistol at arm's length, and fired once into Agnes's face. She fell beside me like a bale of wet straw tossed from the barn loft, her blood pouring out on the tiles.

I raised the shotgun, but my mind could not manage my body. The man grabbed the barrel, pushed it aside, then jerked it forward with me attached, like a little fish on a cane pole. With his other hand, he swatted me like a bee from a picnic ham. My jaw cracked as I fell back deep into the dark pantry against a shelf of cookbooks, scattering them on the floor.

Maggie screamed upstairs as she'd never screamed before, even when she broke her leg in three places at the church social running a foot race. The scream floated in the air, and then the house went quiet. Someone had shut off the truck engine.

The men set to work like it was sheep shearing day, everyone knowing what to do. The driver who shot Father in the neck was in charge.

"Get the good stuff," he said. "Forget the worthless little things. Set nothing on the floor; hoist it right to the truck bed. That's good boys."

I hugged my knees and leaned against the broken shelf hanging lopsided on the wall. The guns were gone, and I was a little girl again. My jaw throbbed.

The driver circulated among the men as they spilled out the contents of drawers, admired paintings on the walls and examined Father's fly rod which hung over the fireplace. When all was working smoothly, the driver stepped back from the action, rubbing his chin like he'd completed one more phase of the job. Blood seeped from a gash in his arm, but he paid it no mind. Like Father, he would finish the job first, then wash up later in the mudroom. He pushed one man towards the downstairs bedroom.

"Only the valuables," he repeated like his men couldn't think for themselves. Still, they looked like they'd done this before. It wasn't necessary to explain what was valuable. Everything was; Father's rugby trophy he'd won in college in Cape Town in 1984; the ostrich feather duster mum brought from South Africa, her silk housecoat she bought in London. All of it was valuable.

When they took the TV, the photo of grandma and grandpa's 50th wedding anniversary slid off the top and fell to the floor, but the glass didn't break, saved by the carpet which I vacuumed a thousand times.

A new man came in, winded. He had searched Father's body. I knew because he tossed his gold pocket watch to the driver before hopping nimbly onto the truck to give the load some order. Now that the number two had arrived, the driver turned his attention up the stairs, as a young boy appeared from nowhere and stood beside him. They had the same space between their front teeth, the same angry nose, a father and his son.

The boy might have been twelve or he might have been sixteen. He dressed in a glittered t-shirt which said '*Ariwa* - The Africa Connection. Kinshasa January 1999.' He had little scars covering his face and sweat on his lip.

As the driver headed took the stairs, he said, "Don't let that girl wiggle free." He pointed to the pantry. "Keep her in there till I come back for her. Do it right and you'll get some too."

He ascended upward. Before disappearing, he unbuckled his belt. I couldn't hear Maggie anymore.

The boy came at me and pushed me back further into the pantry. I felt dizzy like when I drank a full glass of Champaign at Annela De Jager's wedding. I rubbed my jaw as the men yanked out the computer and passed it to the truck, then the fax machine, then the rocking chair Mum sat in while she nursed me and Maggie.

I sat on a stool which I'd used to reach the guns. The boy leaned against the door. I saw he held a machete.

"Is that for me?" I wondered. Maggie screamed a piercing scream, maybe from pain or fear or both. I tried to imagine what they were doing to her. I was almost sure it had something to do with the belt I'd seen the driver unbuckling. I wanted to save Maggie, but I first needed a plan.

I looked at the boy again. "What's your name?" I asked.

"Shut up," he replied. "Don't talk." He brandished the machete.

I saw now he was young, more twelve than sixteen, and not

bright. Girls can tell when a boy opens his mouth if he's bright or stupid. By hearing a boy speak two words, a girl can tell lots about him. This boy wasn't bright. I was sure of it.

I needed a weapon. There was another gun on the shelf above the pickle jars, but it hadn't been fired in years. Father said it was a souvenir from the Boer Wars.

I could throw something. Flour from the bin. The flour scoop. It was metal, but light and not sharp. I closed my eyes and counted to ten. When I opened them again, I felt better. Not dizzy or confused. I knew many things. I knew Father was shot. I knew Mum was far away. I knew Fibian and the maids were dead. I knew Maggie was being hurt. I knew I would be hurt next.

I looked at the machete. The boy glanced frequently over his shoulder to observe the loading, and to listen for sounds of Maggie upstairs. That machete would be my weapon. The boy was not a regular member of this gang. Something he was about to do made him nervous. I noticed the hand without the machete was on his crotch. He began rubbing himself through his buttoned pants.

He saw me watching. "Stand up," he said to me.

I stood. My white socks were splashed with beet juice, darker red than Agnes's blood, almost purple.

"Turn," he said.

I turned but saw - just before he disappeared from my periphery - that he was fiddling with the buttons on the front of his pants.

"Lift your skirt," he said.

"What?" I didn't expect that.

"Lift your skirt," he said louder and banged the machete against the doorframe.

I lifted my skirt in front, then all the way around, front and back. I was wearing blue cotton underpants which could be worn swimming or running a race without thought of impropriety. I stood still. A minute passed, maybe two. Then I heard the sound of the machete as it was placed on the box of canning jars stacked by the door, a sound of opportunity.

I drew a breath.

Then came another sound, a welcome one. Zachary's *bakkie* was revving up the drive. He would bring his gun. He would save Maggie.

As he neared the house, Zachary shouted Maggie's name. She screamed his name in reply. Flesh hit flesh. A gun was fired. My skirt fell back in place as I turned back to see the boy, bent away, stooping over, buttoning his pants. The machete lay on the box of jars as I had imagined.

In one stride I was there. The boy peered up at me as I grasped the silver blade in both hands. He flushed, embarrassed; I'd caught him buttoning his pants. I thought of Father, blood perhaps still pouring from his neck, and I hated this scar-faced boy. I swung. His hand came up without its fingers. Sharper than any knife in our house, I swung again.

It went deep, cutting diagonally across the face, finding a line from the upper left temple to the right edge of the mouth into the jawbone. It sliced the nose diagonally at the bridge but left both eyes uncut. I tried to hold on as he fell, but it had embedded into bone. I let go. The boy went to his knees, took a moment to contemplate these new circumstances, then threw himself hard against the floor. His legs kicked out a series of quick baby steps to get away. The hand with fingers still held the buttons of his pants.

I ran out the back door. Zachary raised his gun but saw it was me, and went down to one knee. I fell into him, cuddling close. I turned to look back at the house. Against a stack of firewood sat the man posted guard with a red wound in the centre of his chest.

"Hey, Zach," I said shyly, shocked more by the lifted skirt than by the machete buried in the boy's bloody face.

"What's happening inside, Jane?" said Zachary, nervous and intense.

"There were three loading the truck. And two upstairs with Maggie. They're hurting her. One is the boss."

"How many guns?"

"I don't know." I shrugged, then thought again. "Two, maybe three."

He nodded. "You wait by the jeep," he said. "I'm going for Maggie."

"Is Father dead?" I asked, matter of fact.

Zach nodded again. "Fibian too. Sons of bitches."

"I killed a little one," I said. "In the pantry. He made me lift my skirt."

"Serves him right, squirt." He patted my head. His fingers twitched on his gun. He signalled for me to go to the jeep. He took several steps to the house, looking back at me once.

"Kill 'em, Zachary," I said.

He entered the back door.

I got into the back seat, figuring Zach would drive and Maggie would insist on the front passenger seat. I found a blanket and put it around me even though it was warm. I covered my head with it, but took it off and sat up straight when shots started again.

There was more gunfire, more shouts. A man came out the front door like he stepped on a nail, hopping three times like a *duikier*. He turned, falling, pointing a pistol back towards the house. He fired twice into the trees and was blown over like a cardboard clown. He landed on his back in the flower bed, crushing Mum's chrysanthemums and the little white picket fence that was supposed to keep rabbits out.

More gunfire. I nearly lost interest. I stared out the window at the baobab tree behind the pump house. Two *go way birds* called to each other, or perhaps to the whole outside world, "Go way! Go way!" making more sense than what I'd seen inside.

If a strange man came out towards the *bakkie*, I'd run across the field. If Zach came out, I'd do whatever he said. I liked Zach even though he made my sister act dumb.

Finally Zach came. He was carrying Maggie, swollen and bloody around her face, wrapped in a sheet. She looked like she was sleeping. There was blood on Zach's right leg, more blood on his hip. He was pale, and his eyes held a look of anger.

He set Maggie in the passenger seat and kissed the top of her head.

"Don't leave," she moaned.

"I won't leave you, Maggie," said Zach.

He opened my door and leaned in close.

"Get my gun upstairs," he whispered, "and bring it back to me now. Then go back and get your sister some clothes. Bring a pullover too. I'll help her get dressed. You have five minutes to get everything you think is important to you and your family. One suitcase. You won't ever come back here again."

I never did.

CANINE EFFECTS ON THE PRICE OF WATER

I stirred a tiny fire back to life. In stillness I watched my daughter sleeping, beautiful in the flickering glow. As the sun's rays came through the entrance to our cave, her loveliness amplified with the dawn. The strain of the last two years had not yet taken up residence in her features. It was a source of pride for me that I sired such a beauty. In normal times, beauty is a ticket for success. In wartime, one's ability to fight counted much more.

I thought of Eva and my son. She was dead. He was missing, presumed dead, though I denied it. Small comfort to consider him missing. Missing meant captured and captured meant tortured. I wished my Eva had not been so contemptuous, answering the watermen as she did. But I didn't imagine the response for her cheeky reply would come from the butt of a rifle. Worse still, the internal injuries festered in a flood of infection. Our son vanished in the night in search of medicines and failed to return. It was a costly remark, telling the betrayers they were unworthy to piss in the lake they had come to steal. Yet I loved her for it. She had spoken the truth.

Without mercy, we killed the crews of those water trucks. They expected acquiescence and were careless. It was their mistake to shoot the wolf-dog Clara when she growled at their feet. She would not have bitten them without Eva's command. For their iniquities they were paid in a currency of rage I never knew existed. My son became a killer, my daughter a cold-blooded murderer. I monitored the carnage from the high ridge near the mouth of our cave, my long rifle trained on the door of the large tent the fools had erected for shade. I didn't fire a shot but watched instead in cold amazement as my children emerged spattered in blood. My son went down instantly to one knee, withdrew field glasses from his belt, and scanned back along the road towards town. My daughter looked up and signaled; a thumbs up, five fingers, then three, and an index finger across the throat. "We're safe. Eight killed."

We kept their weapons and food and forced the men's bodies and all evidence into the tankers. We drove two hours south and set them ablaze in a stony sheep pasture. We hiked back by night along old trails. Eva's condition worsened while we were away; still, we had no choice but to abandon the house. We moved into the cave and watched from the ridge as a new water crew arrived, this time four trucks, sixteen men, and two armed pick-ups. Undoubtedly cognizant of the misfortune of their colleagues, they burned the barn, killed four *criollo* mares, and butchered two steers.

Our home became their base. I wished we had set the booby traps, but time ran out. We saw one drone circling. It didn't have infrared; if it did we would already be dead. I could bring it down, as it was sluggish and overloaded, a surveillance drone outfitted with a light missile. But one lost drone would be replaced by another, bigger and better. We laid low and worked to keep Eva alive.

When she lost consciousness, my son insisted he go for help. We argued against it, but he left that night while we slept. That was four nights ago, and the last we saw of him. Eva died yesterday. Her daughter and I buried her in a grove of pines near the lake.

The water level was down. With four trucks pumping a steady stream, they made the drive back to the provincial capital to the northeast, pipelining the water to the port and exporting it in giant plastic bags. These were towed behind sea-faring tugs to the thirsty people of the north. My thoughts were only of my grief, but my daughter burned with rage. She laid out her plan to sabotage the pumping operation.

"Can't we rest for a day?" I asked her. "Out of respect for your mother."

"Do you think Mother would give these bastards a free day? She'd kill them herself."

"So be it," I capitulated. "Explain again. I'll help."

She would distract the pumpers by fouling the intake where the big hose ran into the deepest part of the lake. She'd swim there in the evening when the watermen were feasting on their *asado* of roasted meat from the butchered steers. This had become a ritual. The men loved their meat, paired with wines from our cellar.

Once the intake was obstructed, we would hide in the trees along the road, watching for weakness. Sixteen were too many to fight at once. But we had killed eight before and could do it again, she assured me.

"Your brother isn't here," I argued.

"But you are," she spit back. "I can't watch while these men steal our lake. They are the enemy. They must die."

We would have to kill quickly before they could respond. Aside from two on the armored trucks, they were engineers and technical workers, not fighters. But some carried guns and knew how to use them, and we were only two.

I'd been the Cassandra, warning about the militarization of the country to the north, their arbitrary use of military power. I predicted they'd come for our water, more prized than oil. But even those who listened felt it was futile to resist. The pumping began on a large scale in the Aquifer. But small outfits like this went out on their own to suck up rivers and lakes, wherever water was fresh.

In fading light, my daughter swam to the center of the lake. She made hardly a ripple. I watched from the thicket. The men were drinking raucously, unaware that two rebels were scheming their bloody deaths. The motor hummed smoothly as the trucks filled. The men devoured their meat, and my daughter swam silently to shore. Soon the motor burped and began to whine as the mud and gravel she had forced into the pipe reached the pump's chambers.

It was ten minutes before they noticed the straining motor. They reversed the pump's direction, restarted it repeatedly, then gathered at the boat shed on the shoreline, scratching their heads and debating what could have gone wrong.

I moved behind the house and set it afire. I spiked the gun in one of the armored trucks and inspected the second. I rolled it into position. I pulled back on the bolt, and the large caliber mounted weapon was ready for business.

As the fire began to consume the house, there were shouts from the men. Several ran closer to see the smoke and flames. I shot them with my deer rifle. As I killed them, my daughter sprinted closer to the main gathering standing near the pump. I shifted to the mighty Browning in the truck bed and watched my daughter disappear behind the shed. She carried a huge knife and had two pistols in her waistband. The group had not yet identified the source of the rifle fire. I shot the two who stood nearest me, still using my own rifle. I saw my daughter spring from behind the shed where she slit two throats, then drew both pistols and began firing. We managed to slay every one before a weapon could be drawn against us.

I was unsure how many remained, but two came out the burning house, now well-ablaze. One held a sub-machine gun and began firing madly. As he ran, I fired with the unfamiliar gun. I hoped my daughter saw him coming. She did. Rather than take cover, she stood her ground, aimed, and hit him in the forehead. The second man dropped his weapon and raised his hands. I killed him where he stood.

We met at the front of the house and stood watching our home burn. It was too late to rescue anything. She put her arm on my shoulder.

As part of the roof collapsed, she said, "We must go."

"Right. But where?" I asked.

"The Pools. They'll send the dogs next."

"Dogs?" I asked.

"Don't think. Let's move."

At the cave, we gathered a few items into packs. We selected weapons we could carry and broke stocks and scattered magazines of those we could not. In fifteen minutes, we were walking the lake trail to higher elevation, deep cover, perhaps a few more days of freedom. We headed towards the Glacier Pools. We had friends there.

Just before losing sight of the road, we saw a caravan stop at the entrance to our *estancia*. Soldiers pulled back tarpaulins and began offloading cargo. They were unleashing the war dogs. Six mechanical animals cocked their heads and sniffed the air. One by one, they embarked on their terrible trot. Robotic. Silent. Relentless.

They were headed in our direction.

TIME BOMB

My name is Rashid, but I am called Albert. I am invisible. I see through walls and over hills. I see behind faces and float like a leaf above the deep currents which others call life. Yet I have no life of my own. I only observe. I observe life in the City.

I'm Saudi, but my documents say I am Lebanese. I have always envied the Lebanese, so smart, so social, and always active in their communities. Family is important if you are Lebanese. Relationships matter. But these are things which were never mine. Family. Relationships. Community. It's too late for me. The world is already tainted, like a defiled maiden. Like spoiled milk.

The Lebanese once had it all. They had Beirut. As a child I saw posters of its beautiful beaches and skyline, and ever since I believed that Beirut was heaven. In my next life, I will be born Lebanese in Beirut, before politics and war turn it into a ghetto. I will have family and friends, stature in my community. Respect. Perhaps I will have children. Who knows? Not even I can see clearly into the next life.

I met the American couple when it became necessary to move

out of my flat. The government insisted that housing should be made more efficient in the City, declaring that there must be at least one person for each room residing in any house or apartment. At that time I lived in a large flat with two bedrooms and several other living spaces which could easily have been converted to bedrooms. The government would certainly proclaim them as such and force me to share.

On a Monday morning, I received a visit from a government housing inspector. By Tuesday three people I had never met arrived to occupy my second bedroom. The husband smelled of sweat, the wife didn't cover her head, even less her fat thighs and huge bosoms. The baby screamed all hours of the day and night. They invaded my kitchen and overtook my refrigerator, filling it with smelly and unidentifiable ointments and sauces. The arrangement lasted only a week. I moved out before even beginning my search for an alternative place to live.

I found the American couple almost immediately and moved in with them. They were well-off, and their apartment was opulent by most standards. I never collected material possessions – an envelope filled with cash made so much more sense to me – so my small bag of jeans, underwear, and a few shirts were swallowed up immediately in their large spare bedroom, now mine. The Americans had decided not to wait for a stranger to be assigned to them. They selected me while they still had a choice.

There was the formality of an interview. I can be charming, and my intellect is quickly apparent by my speech and vocabulary. I can talk about anything, which is not to say that I do. They spoke with me for only a few minutes before they looked at each other and nodded. They would have given me free rent if I'd insisted. Instead, I proffered a reasonable sum, and we shook hands on the arrangement. It is best not to owe or to be owed anything these days when the future is so uncertain.

He had no work permit. He was an elementary school teacher

with no fixed position. Instead, he taught as a substitute at two of the City's international schools on a cash basis. He also gave private English lessons to children who needed remedial help, and to business people who wanted to improve their conversation skills, either to pick up business opportunities or to pick up girls in the tourist bars. Both opportunities and tourists were becoming rare, so the competition must have been stiff.

The woman wore the pants in the relationship. She was a contract manager for a big oil firm, and made ten times what he did, not to mention housing, car, pension, and benefits paid by the company. She was very sharp – I could see that – but something was missing. There were no kids, which was a point of friction between them. She couldn't be bothered with children, but he was born to be a papa. If men had been given birthing hips, he would have been blessed with a prominent set. But the issue of children was never discussed. Still, I knew. I read people. Their words and the interaction of their bodies told me these things that day.

There was more that it told me. They were from the southern United States, probably Texas. She was a careerist, still young but effective in climbing corporate ladders. She knew the finer points of the local culture, knew a great deal about the socialists running the government, knew how some things worked and some things didn't work in the City. She didn't mind having the upper hand in the relationship but was ashamed that her husband felt so inadequate. She was passionate, not about her job but her career. He on the other hand had a look of fear in his eyes so common to people these days. These were challenging times. The writing was on the wall, and people were beginning to read it. You can only step over so many starving beggars on the street before the reality hits you that there are a lot of starving beggars on the street. What is amazing is how long it takes for most people to notice.

He noticed. She either didn't notice or didn't care. She had other concerns, and her position of privilege insulated her from the brutality on the streets. She had something to prove. Maybe it was the money. Money blinds a lot of people; sex, money, power, the three big corruptors. The money she was paid was certainly good, but she was just getting started. If she proved tough enough, big bucks were just around the corner.

Her company had a reputation as a big polluter and was hated by the environmentalists, especially here in the City. Security was extreme; to get in the corporate office was like getting into the Pentagon unless you were an employee or a spouse. For the first year on the job, the woman served as an aide on the legal team fighting an immense lawsuit demanding billions in compensation for environmental damages. An entire province in the interior of the country had been all but declared unfit for habitation after the water table was polluted with oil and toxic chemicals. While the case was battled to a standstill in the international courts, the company changed hands. The new owners returned to do business under a different name. She carved a place for herself in the restructured organization, negotiating a contract on the construction of a controversial pipeline. When she succeeded, she was promoted and put in charge of buying rights for shale oil fracking in dozens of drilling properties scattered throughout the interior.

These were challenging times, and social unrest was everywhere in the City. There were too many people, and people were the one thing no one needed anymore. Why care about people? Why reach out to save a brother when his salvation might mean your demise? He competed with you for water, space, food, and fuel. Most recently he competed with you for shade. The temperatures were high, and electricity in the City was turned off more than it was on. The cost was too much for most to afford, but even with money, there was often no electricity to buy. This made people unhappy and irritable and often vicious.

A beautifully flowered shade tree in a park across the street became a scene of frequent violence. Families and clans and gangs and stragglers came to the City from the even hotter temperatures in the northern interior and fought for the respite of the shade of this lovely tree in the park. What started as pushing and intimidation led to knife fights to the death, all for a piece of shade. I watched from my window sometimes when the sun wasn't too hot to stand near it. It was a dynamic struggle; one group took possession of the space, while another stood by at a distance, waiting for an opportunity to strike.

Everyone fought to survive in the City. Road rage killed hundreds every week, despite fewer cars on the road. It was a bad time to be a human being. We had already made it miserable for the plants and animals. Now it was our turn.

The tension took a toll on my flatmates and their relationship. They fought over everything, sometimes over matters so subtle that even I could not decipher what had turned one against the other. It could be something as ridiculous as the choice of cup used to serve coffee or the brand of laundry soap selected at the kiosk. There was an endless stream of reasons to fight. But two things never came up, the two reasons which I would have expected. One was their barren marriage. The other was the immorality of her work.

People who understood the dystopian scenes played out daily before their eyes knew that the energy companies were responsible. Worse still, those same companies were scrambling to extract the maximum oil and gas and coal from their vast reserves and pocket their fortunes before governments found the will to control the release of carbon into the atmosphere. The corporate spin was that the world was clamoring for energy; they were merely supplying it. It was factually proven that average global temperatures had already risen three degrees and were headed upward. It would soon hit six, even if drilling stopped today. The world was coming to a boil.

I never interfered with the couple's disagreements. When an argument erupted, I rose quietly and left the room. I found both of the combatants tiresome in their bickering. Neither was right.

Neither could stop. Nothing was ever settled. It was hell, but it was a familiar hell they had created for themselves.

I had sexual relations with the female one night. He went out with friends after a bitter argument during dinner. She came to my room later to apologize for making me uncomfortable. I was lying naked on the bed, reading a newspaper. I rose to put on my slip and a pair of shorts, but she came to me before I knew it. She kissed me once and pushed me back on the bed. I asked for none of it, nor did I refuse her. I had American women before, and she was by comparison more passionate and skilled than the others. She left once we had finished, and never spoke of it again. At least not to me.

They separated soon after. He moved in with a friend and rarely came around. I feared that the government would put someone else with the woman and me, but as with so many socialist policies, the government lost its fire in squeezing people into available housing against their wishes. No one came to take the man's place. I thought too that my relationship with the woman would change now that the husband was away, but it didn't. I gave her no sign of deeper interest, and she was hands-full with work and responsibility.

The man came to the flat one day when the woman was not home, and I let him in.

"Should you be here?" I asked.

"Why not?" he asked. "This is my house too."

"How are you doing?" I asked him.

"I'm fine," he said. "As well as can be expected."

What did that mean, I wondered? No one expected much these days. Stay alive, maybe. Eat something every day. That was enough for most.

"Did you sleep with her?" he asked me out of the blue.

"I did," I responded honestly.

"I thought so," he said, head down.

"Did she tell you?"

"Not in so many words," he said. It was awkward, but I felt no remorse.

"Are you angry?" I asked.

"I'm angry about so many things," he said. "This is just one more."

Then he came to me. I prepared to defend myself, but instead, he leaned in and kissed my mouth.

"What was that?" I asked, surprised.

"I don't know," he said. "I guess I wanted to do that for a long time."

"Why?" I asked him, wiping the wetness from my lips.

"I like you, I guess. I don't know anything about you," he said, "but I like you. I find that there are so few people that I can say that about these days."

"I know. It isn't easy, is it," I offered.

"What do you mean?" he asked me.

"Getting along," I said. "It isn't easy getting along."

"No," he said. "But you are comfortable. Like an old jacket. If I knew you better perhaps I wouldn't like you so much."

We stood a moment in silence. "I need a favor," he said.

"What do you need?"

"I need … look, I know this is a strange request," he said.

It figured that he would back his way into it. "Go ahead," I encouraged him once. "The worst I can say is no."

"No," he corrected me. "There are worse things you can say than no."

"Then ask me. I'm afraid I have no idea what you will ask."

"Do you know someone … who knows someone, who knows how to make a bomb?"

This time I went to him. I grabbed his collar and pulled him close. My right thumb was pressed to his left eye, one thrust away from blinding him. My left hand at his throat could paralyze him in a split second. He was big but soft. He was weak and had no will to use what little strength he had. I felt no respect for him. But like him, there were very few people in the world who I did respect. I could think of no one.

"Why do you come to me with this?" I demanded.

"I thought you might know?" he grunted.

"What have you heard about me?"

"Ouch!" he complained and tried feebly to pull away. "It was just a feeling."

"Tell me about this feeling? Is it because I'm ... Lebanese?"

"No. I forgot that you were Lebanese," he said. "I can't explain it. I just felt that you were someone to ask."

"Who else knows about this? Who put you up to this?"

"Nobody. You're the first person I've ever mentioned this to."

"And this is what? Your plan to take over the government?"

"God no," he almost laughed. "I hate the government but have no intention to take it over. I could do no better."

That seemed at least honest. "Then what?"

"People are hurting the planet. I intend to stop them."

"What about your wife?"

"Ha? What about her?"

"Will you kill her too? Isn't she hurting the planet?"

He didn't answer. He seemed stunned by the idea as if it had never crossed his mind until now. But it could have been subconscious. His interest in saving the world was perhaps only a way to get revenge on a wife who kicked him out.

"Help me," he pleaded pathetically. "Help me if you can. Please."

I had to stop and think. And you too perhaps. You may have been wondering, what is it that I do? I will not tell you, as you have no reason to know. But I will tell you that I too have people to whom I must give an accounting. I may be invisible. I may not be alive, only an observer. That doesn't mean I answer to no one.

I had a mission, and my mission involved explosives. While I didn't know how this man could have guessed my vocation, he came to me at an opportune moment, a moment when I needed to make a showing, test a product, prove a theory. This man might be exactly what I needed to climb the very modest little ladder on which I had positioned myself.

"We will talk," I said. "But first you will tell me everything. Everything you plan to do. Everyone you've spoken to. What you hope to accomplish, and when and where and who will be involved. Do you understand?" He nodded and I released him.

We began to meet late at night, not for secrecy but for the cooler temperatures. We walked and talked, and became almost friends. He told me what he hoped to do. I told him how to do it. His agenda was not mine, but there was a critical overlap. When it felt right, we set a date.

He came to me the morning of the day he planned to teach the world a lesson, for which I had provided the lesson plan.

I saw her earlier that same morning. Our hands brushed together as we placed our dishes into the sink after a small breakfast, which we had eaten alone in our separate rooms.

"Hello," she said.

"Hello," I answered.

"I've been wanting to talk to you," she said. She appeared shy.

"That would be fine," I said, and her eyes brightened a shade. "When would you like to talk?"

"Tonight after work if you will be home."

I said I would be, and our conversation ended. She left for work. An hour later, the buzzer rang and I let the American man in. He came heavily up the stairs; the elevator hadn't worked in months. I offered him a glass of water, then took him to my room and placed a backpack on his shoulders. He said it would be so hot out there and I said I'd thought about that, and had placed the whole rig on ice in a cooler on the floor of my closet. The ball bearings would be icy cold so that the vest would not feel so hot on his back. He thanked me for my thoughtfulness.

I showed him again the new trigger mechanism which I had made and said it was common that people got distracted, perhaps bumped by a stranger, slipped on dog shit, or tripped over an unconscious street vendor who collapsed on the sidewalk. The mechanism was safe as long as you didn't release the button too soon, but once you pushed it in to activate, there was no going back. The backpack was made so that it could not be removed without releasing the trigger. That was how it was meant to work, and there was no secret way to back out.

He said he understood. Then he said something else. "I suppose you wonder why I didn't intervene before. Why I waited until now to do something. This isn't an excuse I'm offering, but I want you to know."

"Know what?" I asked.

The fear had gone from his eyes. "The money was so good," he said. "It overcomes any moral objections about what you're doing. I too am guilty. I liked the money so much."

"I understand," I said, and I did. Money overcomes many things, even the willing and wanton destruction of the earth, it seems.

He left. I packed my small bag and left my key on the table by the door. On the same table stood a wedding picture of the once happy couple. I placed it face down next to my key.

There was a chance he would falter, then come back here to me for rescue.

And the trigger? There was a secret release. I would not be here to show him how it could be done. No one else would know.

CLIFF WILLIAMSON

HEART 4.0

I completed The Cultural History of Marriage Short Course. It was elementary for me. I read the pages of source material and when finished I correctly answered the study questions. It took less than one hour. I would have completed it faster but I was simultaneously performing my routine work responsibilities. I was new. I have since learned it is not recommended that I apply myself to non-essential activities when engaged in work at the Factory. It could distract me from my primary function, cause an accident, or produce service failures. I completed the course at a time when I was still undergoing efficiency adjustments, some of them major, so I was not penalized for this small transgression. I reported it promptly, and have suffered no corrective measures. 'My slate is clean,' you would say, though I have no actual slate in my working inventory.

I am uncertain what caused me to enroll in that particular course of study. Seeing me you may wonder the same. I would not appear to be 'the marrying kind.' Yet I harbor no regrets for the experience. I remember every word of the discourse and continue to find the phenomenon of marriage intriguing.

I learned that marriage took different forms throughout history. It has *evolved,* you would say. Originally, marriage was an arrangement of convenience for genetic survival, or what you technically refer to as 'procreation.' But few formalities existed in those early days. The female had no voice in the matter of who she married, or at what age. A physically dominant male simply took possession of her and that was that.

'End of story,' as you would say.

Thereafter, families soon began selling their daughters to be wed to a suitable man in exchange for a dowry. Only much later did women gain autonomy over their lives and bodies and influence the choice of mate and time of pairing. But this took many years. Centuries, in fact. It was a *process*.

The rite of marriage was always restricted to a single species, the *homo sapiens*. Other creatures formed relationships, such as elephant, gorilla, and albatross. Sometimes these relationships were monogamous, but marriage as a ritual was always species specific, and always to the opposite gender. Until the 1900's marriage occurred between members of the same race with few exceptions. Interracial marriage became legally accepted in advanced society in the 1960s, but acceptance by the public came slowly. Gay marriage was not legalized until much later, after the New Millennium, and there was great controversy surrounding it long after it became legally permitted. After the First Century of the New Millennium, individuals who broke these social barriers were sometimes considered heroes.

Perhaps I too will be thought a hero one day.

These are not the best of times on earth nor are they the best of times in the Factory. As the Director often states in his speeches to our staff, we are locked in a struggle for survival. Success depends on every member of society working together in unselfish collaboration.

But if you will permit me a polite observation, there is hope that a corner has been turned, as you would say. I don't mean turning a corner as when you are conducting a vehicle. I mean 'turning over a new leaf.'

I like many of your expressions such as these. They humor me. Humor me = LIKE.

By 'turning a corner' or 'turning over a new leaf,' both the corner and the leaf to which I refer is a statistical one. After years of misery, there have been signs of stabilization in some of earth's most worrisome trends. Sea Level Rise has nearly stopped, less than a millimeter a year for three years in succession. Average Global Temperature has steadied, and in fact, reversed in some of the lands which remain above water. Polar Ice is beginning to form once again. It is hoped this year's newly formed ice may endure into the coming season. Carbon particulate has fallen below 550 ppm, a first in more than fifty years.

Hooray for us. The Director is careful not to show excitement, but I am 74% certain he is pleased.

There is reason for hope, and hope leads to good things. With hope, we care about the future. With hope, we see a return to concerts and theaters, hosting of parties, and the celebration of special days with feasts and special cakes with candles. With hope humans hum or whistle as they work. With hope, humans find time for love. They have intimate talks about starting families and building partnerships.

Partnerships such as marriage, for example.

My name is Peter. I originate from Cincinnati and currently reside in Buffalo, the old state of New York. Buffalo is an Industrial Community, a place to live and work. In Buffalo, you can find everything important that exists on the earth. That is what humans from Buffalo say. 'If you can't find it in Buffalo, it is not worth having.'

It is a small joke.

I work at the Factory. My job is not interesting, but I am pleased to have a job so that I may serve an important function for The Good of All Things. I am now a welder, but with minor adjustments, I am capable of completing any task. I am told that I am resourceful and creative. It adds to my value. Value is good.

If you prefer to think mathematically, you can express it like this:

Resourcefulness = R Value = V P = Peter

So, if ....

R = V and

P = R

Then ...

P = V

This makes me proud.

I will tell you about Orchidea. She too works at the Factory. In a way, you could say she is my superior. This does not mean she is better than me though I believe this may be true. It only means that her name appears above mine in the organigram posted on the wall of the assembly room outside the Resource Hall.

Orchidea has never mentioned that she is superior to me. I am not sure if she thinks or cares about it. I may ask her one day.

Orchidea is a fine subject for observation. I have been cautioned about observing things, as observation can serve as a distraction from my duties. I am 95.6% certain that the quality of my work does not suffer when I am observing Orchidea, but I keep this concept active as a warning so that if it does begin to affect the quality of my work, I can make adjustments to correct my behavior.

I hope that does not happen, as I draw pleasure from observing Orchidea. She is an exceptional specimen. Perhaps it sounds funny to call Orchidea a specimen. If so I apologize. 'No offense intended,' as you would say.

We met two years ago when the supply train I was conducting was waylaid in the main corridor. There was a spill on the shop floor directly in my path. I could have continued on my way but my instructions were explicit. Even if it were possible to pass over or through the obstacle or substance in the intended pathway, one should pause and consult with a superior to be certain no further damage will result. I therefore applied the hand brake and called the nearest D11 to render assistance.

Orchidea was the nearest D11 and she came instantly, as was her duty. She was a responsible D11. She placed herself directly in front of the train and asked what I thought I was doing. I giggled slightly because her idea that I was thinking about what I was doing sounded odd to me. I was not thinking about what I was doing; I was doing. Perhaps you will wish to research the CN1231 Manual, Section 3 Paragraph 9 Parts a, b, and c to understand why I find this humorous. It is not required that you conduct research at this time, but if you did, you would get a clear idea of 'what I am driving at.' That is another funny expression if you ask me, which 'if you ask me' is another one. If something is funny it is funny if you ask me or if you don't. Don't ask me why. Ha Ha.

Orchidea got angry when I giggled, and I found her worthy to observe as her anger escalated within her. Her expression changed and her skin turned pink. I sensed her heart rate increase and felt her temperature rise. I found this experience fascinating and exquisite.

That is an exquisite word. Exquisite. I use it when I can, though there are few occasions to do so during our Struggle.

I knew also that a co-worker's anger was not something to ignore so I explained myself to her.

"There is a liquid substance on the pathway which may cause damage to this vehicle or result in an accident if I pass through it. I am 82% certain it is BLU20009XLV grease, the principal lubricant in the EverTrue 4M Drill Press on your left. The high pitched sound I am hearing and you are not may be from a friction point in the left rear flywheel bearing of the Drill Press. There is a 13% chance the substance is not grease but instead is hydraulic fluid from the rocker arm elevator hose on the same machine, but ... "

Orchidea shouted, "Fuck the grease." She stepped aside and pointed ahead. "Move it!" she shouted.

I did as I was told and drove forward. I saw in my left periphery sector that she was smiling as I passed. She was smiling at me.

I do not recall seeing Orchidea before the moment of the grease spill, but after that moment I saw her nearly every day. First, it was 'by accident', which means at random or by chance – it does not mean we were involved in an accident. One day I saw her walking through the cafeteria doors, and the next day I saw her entering the washroom. Later I saw her riding on the hitch bar of a skid loader driven by a colleague with red hair which is against the rules. I thought it was funny and harmless so I set my Report-An-Error Protocol to override. I am 78% certain she looked at me and saw me observing as she rode by. Her hair was loose and it flew behind her like a flag. This made me feel … exquisite.

On that day I chose to make Orchidea my Number One and I calculated there was a 98.7% chance she would always remain my Number One. The probability that she would choose to make me her Number One was far less. It was unlikely, about 1.07%. But I did not feel discouraged. I decided to inform her I had selected her as my Number One, but I found it challenging to arrange an encounter in which I could advise her of my choice.

To survive on earth we must work every day. As the Director says, work is our only true alternative if we are to endure in these harsh conditions we have inherited. But because there are so many demands on our time, there were few opportunities to meet someone in settings other than the workplace. Where and when could two individuals meet to have intimate talks about starting a family and building a partnership? How would I be able to arrange an encounter with Orchidea to speak with her about this subject?

There was an assembly on Recognition Day, and as he did every year on Recognition Day, the Director made a speech to all of us in the Resource Hall. I did not plan to touch Orchidea there, but I had trained myself to prepare in case a chance encounter took place.

I posed in the back of the room where I usually do near the exhaust fans. I could hear the Director speaking even if the fans ran noisily. This made space available for others in positions closer to the Director so they could hear him speak his important words about dedication and sacrifice and struggle and teamwork. When he began talking about the coming storms, Orchidea interrupted his words. She came loudly through the double doors together with a colleague with red hair. I could see the sweat on her lip and moisture spots on her clothing under her armpits where Orchidea sometimes emitted water for cooling if the temperature was too hot, if the work was demanding, or if she was uneasy about something. The temperature was not hot that day so I know Orchidea was either working hard, or she was uneasy. Her hands were not dirty and she was not wearing protective gear, so it was 84.2% likely that she was uneasy.

She stood close to me, and I confirmed her heart rate was 8 beats above her normal 82 bpm, and her skin temperature was 2 degrees higher than her normal temperature. I moved closer. I heard her whisper to her colleague with red hair.

She said, "Goddamn Cecil. Next time I'll kill him."

"Little fucker," answered the girl with red hair. Cecil was a man in our work circle who was known for playing tricks. I did not think his tricks were funny but Cecil laughed after his tricks, so he believed his tricks were funny. Cecil's tricks often meant someone would get grease or oil or water on their clothes or in their hair. Later I would listen to see if I could learn what was this trick Cecil played on Orchidea and the girl with red hair.

There are many poses available to me when I listened to the Director's speech. One pose was with my arms down by my side. Another pose was with my shoulders rotated outwards, allowing my arms to extend further from my body. The first pose was used when

I moved through narrow passageways. The second pose was used when I performed tasks requiring lateral arm movements. I slowly shifted my pose from the narrow profile to the lateral profile. I did so at a slow speed with no audible sound. My left hand came into contact with the right hand or Orchidea. My contact was minimal, no more than 10^{-5} Newtons, which is no more than a sunflower pushes as it leans towards the light. Her hand was warm and soft. She did not notice, or if she did she did not speak out about it nor move away. I listened to the Director speak, standing there together, touching Orchidea's hand. When he finished, we separated and returned to the work floor.

That was a special day. I will remember the moment of that day as long as I have memory. I have named it 'Hand Hold Day.'

I sought other opportunities to touch Orchidea, but it was not easy. One day Orchidea touched me. I was working on a line with other colleagues when the conveyor stopped. I did not realize my foot was tangled in a mesh net used to pack and ship products to consumers. I did not know it was there. If the mesh had caught on the conveyor, it would have been a serious problem for me.

Orchidea was there immediately. Maybe she was the first one to see the problem and push the emergency stop button. Maybe some other worker saw and reported it. If it was Orchidea, I owe her my life. She withdrew a sharp tool from her belt and stood behind me. She put her hand below my hip and examined me closely.

"What's this, my worker bee? You're a mess. Let's get this off of you before you fly into the hopper like a Jumper!"

I have heard that outside in other lands many committed suicide by jumping off high places or jumping in front of trucks or trains. I was not a Jumper, so I think Orchidea was making a joke. Ha.

She bent down and I could see her exquisite form as she pulled the mesh away and cut me free. She formed a beautiful image for observing as she stood. She wore the Factory uniform, but she wore it more nobly than all others who worked on the floor. A lock of

Orchidea's hair lay against her face. I called this 'Perfect Imperfection,' when Orchidea's hair was out of place but still in exactly the right place for a fine visual impact. Her hands worked like butterflies and as she touched me I could feel that she was both strong and weak, what I have heard some refer to as 'feminine' - strong and weak at the same moment. I only know strong, but I can adjust to 'gentle' which is like weak but not exactly. Feminine is more intriguing than gentle. I regret that I have no feminine settings.

When she finished, she touched me on my buttocks. I reached to touch her on her buttocks to express my thanks, but she moved away.

"Whoa!" she said. "Not so fast, junior!" Then she turned to her colleague and said, "Mr. Horny here tried to touch my ass!"

"Report the bastard," said the girl with the red hair.

"Who knows? I might like it," Orchidea replied.

They walked away laughing. It was perfect. I reflected on how she touched me, and how I moved to touch her in that place where humans act shy called the buttocks. I replayed the memory over and over in my mind. This immediately became another special moment and another special day I keep in my memory. 'Orchidea Saves Peter Day.'

I was assigned to a different assembly line which took me away from Orchidea's supervision. I saw her occasionally but was no longer able to observe her work, watch her interact with her friend with the red hair, or witness her chase Cecil around the tool cabinets with a grease gun, laughing as he ran from her. Still, I generated scenes of break times and lunchtimes spent with her, walking beside her to her home in the barracks, and touching her again.

I knew about sex. I did not complete the Short Course, but I learned things from my curious nature. I knew that sex between Orchidea and me would be mechanical and unconventional the first time. I had no experience but I was resourceful and creative. I was convinced I had the tools and attachments to offer the pleasure a human female would expect from her Number One.

I learned a trick. I will tell you now. Because it was often warm in the Factory, I learned a way to be close to Orchidea. In the season when the sun is closest and shines most directly on the Factory roof, I knew Orchidea would feel discomfort. I knew she did not like it when the Factory was so warm that the machines were sometimes too hot to touch, and the fans that blew air from one side of the assembly area to the other did not make more than 2.5 degrees of difference on Orchidea's exquisite skin. I moved close to her one day and directed a stream of cool air towards the moist area of her shirt beneath her arms. She looked up at me and smiled.

"What are you doing?" she asked with a look of confusion on her face. She raised her arms and rotated slowly in front of the cooling air stream.

"Hey, that feels nice. Who told you to … ahhh!" she said. I knew I was giving her pleasure because a human female will often say 'ahhh' when she feels pleasure. She may also say 'ahhh' when there is a special understanding which occurs, but I think this time it was because of the physical pleasure she felt from the cool air. I am 89% certain she meant 'ahhh' in this way. But I have heard Cecil say that it is hard to know what gives pleasure to a female human, or what they are thinking at any time.

I was out of my work area and left Orchidea to return to my line. Two days later I was reassigned to Orchidea's section. She positioned me next to her own work station. This made me say 'ahhh.' I did not say 'ahhh' but I did think it in my mind.

All through the hot summer Orchidea and I worked together and I was able to watch her exquisite form as she lifted and twisted and cut and packaged. Sometimes she played and gossiped – a funny word used by humans – with her friends, especially the girl with the red hair whose name was Cherry.

Cherry made jokes to Orchidea that I was her Number One, and that she should take me to her barracks after her work shift was over. I would enjoy that but Orchidea did not request me to come.

One day the great storms came, the ones the Director told us about. The Director called us to the Resource Hall for a meeting. He had sweat on his lip and under his arms, but he was not hot. The temperature was dropping fast outside and the Director said we must prepare for the deep cold which was coming. The lights flashed while he spoke. The Resource Hall went dark and emergency power switched on. Orchidea and the girl with red hair screamed.

The storm lasted nine days, first with strong winds, then rain, then snow, then ice, then a tremendous silent freeze which came into the Factory and stopped all machines, all power, and all work which was our responsibility to do.

It was colder than it had ever been before. Ice formed on the machines. Workers broke packing crates and set them on fire to keep warm, but this was not enough. Many collapsed on the floor near the fires.

Orchidea went to her barracks and did not return. I went to find her. I first located her barracks, then I located her room. I went to her bedside as she lay there with many quilts and coats and packing materials on top of her. I touched her cheek and it was cold. It was dangerous for her to be so cold.

I began to generate heat for her. I could only direct it to one part of her at a time, and this was insufficient. Cherry the red-haired girl was in the bed next to Orchidea. But Cherry was cold with ice crystals in her red hair, and her body was stiff. I left Orchidea and went to Cherry. I removed her from her bed and put her on the floor. I did not show caution when I lifted Cherry from the mattress, because she was dead and I did not like Cherry. I was more careful with Cherry's mattress because it would now become Orchidea's mattress.

I lifted the mattress off the bed frame and laid it on the floor. I put three quilts from Cherry's bed on the mattress. I lifted Orchidea from her bed and laid her on the new bed I had prepared. I spread the other covers and extra quilts beside the bed. I must work fast to save Orchidea.

I moved onto the mattress and put myself into the flat pose beside Orchidea. I covered both of us with the quilts. I then set my temperature to high.

Orchidea lay close to me as my warmth raised the temperature around us. It raised the temperature of Orchidea too, her face, her hands and feet, her body.

"Orchidea," I said. "Do you hear me?"

She said nothing.

"Do you feel the warm air I am directing to you?" I asked her.

She did not answer but I heard her breathing. I rolled over into the crawl pose and positioned myself above Orchidea. She lay beneath me. I observed her small clouds of breath. I lowered myself down until we touched. I felt the cold body beneath me but observed that her temperature was rising and her heartbeat was increasing.

"Orchidea?" I called to her. She lay silent.

"Will you be my Number One?" I asked.

"Orchidea," I said again. "Will you be my Number One?"

She was breathing regularly. Her heart made sounds like it was talking to me. I asked the question I wanted to ask for so long.

"Will you marry me?"

No answer came from Orchidea's lips. But she moved. With closed eyes, she turned her face to me. She raised her arms and put them around me. She wrapped her legs around my legs.

"Ahhh," Orchidea said.

Exquisite.

LIVE BY THE SWORD

As I looked out from Athen's Gate over the Pangrati Valley, Silibi's black skin was surprisingly reflective of the morning sunlight that pierced through the few clouds above. I thought the color black absorbed light, yet there she stood, radiating light, not absorbing it, posed like *Amanishakeheto*, the Nubian Warrior Queen.

She protected her eyes with her hand as she studied the expanse laid out before her. 'There. Let's go there,' she said and pointed across the valley. I shaded my own eyes to see what she had indicated. It appeared to be a small café where twenty or so people were gathered in a courtyard beside round tables shaded by a small grove of olive and bitter orange trees. I had to admit, the place looked intriguing. Still, I probed why.

'Why not?' she said. 'It will be a fun ride getting there. It's a destination. A goal. You said we always need a goal, right? That's what you always tell me.'

She was right. I did often say that in my preachy voice. Surprisingly she listened. She was a girl who raised herself from frightened naïf on the back streets in Addis Ababa to become a

Université de Genève graduate. This trip was her graduation gift. She asked for Greece. I complied.

She was a remarkable girl; five languages all spoken like a native, impeccably good taste in fashion, a quick study of any subject put before her, pleasant though somewhat opinionated, and a natural beauty. She had enormous power but didn't yet realize it, something only I seemed to have recognized. I figured I had another two or three months tops before she figured it out, and told me to fuck off. I had invested in her, but she owed me nothing in return. Not even respect. All I did was provide opportunity, a bit of spending money, and I let her go at the world like a pit bull. She did the rest herself. She had the skills, the motivation. I just believed in her. I guess that's worth something, right?

My return on investment was this beautiful woman on my arm, a travel companion, and some cover for my business selling bombs and missiles and military rifles. I had the right connections. I could put my hands on any war-making materiel I wanted, and could sell it for exorbitant sums. It was me who propped up those quickly disappearing failed states, self-made kings, and corrupt politicians. I knew how to find the sweet spot, and I had my special niche. I gathered the table scraps from botched wars and resold them to the vultures who waited in the wings. I was small potatoes, dealing in mere millions instead of billions. It was a living.

But my market was disappearing. Too much transparency these days. Too much surveillance. Too much shared information among the rich countries in the world, the real weapon manufacturers. My golden years were behind me. I was just putting together a few more deals, saving for my retirement.

Silibi thought I sold investment bonds. I planned to let her think that as long as possible. The minute she got downwind of my real job, she would smell the rat I truly was and say goodbye. If she found out too much it would be dangerous to both of us, and I walked a fine line. I knew she was smart when I first took her home.

CANINE EFFECTS ON THE PRICE OF WATER

But it turns out she was much smarter. She worked hard. She learned fast. I just hoped she wouldn't one day playfully snoop through my emails and phone records. I was a good protector of my privacy, but one little fuck-up could expose me, and then I would have a mess to clean up. That mess might include Silibi. That would make me sad. I would never have admitted it to anyone, leastwise myself. Not until this trip did I realize that I had feelings for her. I guessed she was coming to know it too.

I wasn't used to that kind of intimacy. Any kind of intimacy. Not since my parents were killed in the Argentine Dirty Wars of the '70s. I had learned to be alone, to work alone, to think, and survive as one.

Sometimes I thought I meant more to her than the sugar I provided her. Sometimes I was convinced I was nothing but. She was young. She didn't know what she wanted. And me? I found it harder every day to get out of bed. The war wounds and the bar fights were catching up to me. My self-abuse was taking its toll. And I was too old for this young man's game.

A Tarot reader in Marrakech once told me I would die young. 'How young,' I asked? 'Sure you want to know?' she asked me, looking up at me with smoky eyes. I nodded yes. 'Fifty-nine,' she said. 'How? I asked her without thinking. 'Violently,' she came back immediately. 'You will die violently at fifty-nine.' It felt like a punch in the gut. 'Want to know more?' she asked. 'Will it help me avoid it?' I asked. 'No,' she said. 'Forget it then.' I walked out and got drunk. I'm not sure I've been completely sober since.

I would turn fifty-nine in a few days. I told Silibi we'd come here both to celebrate my birthday and her graduation. A twofer, I said. In reality, I came here to meet a buyer, but the celebration on a Greek Island was good back story. We were scheduled to sail tomorrow to Santorini, then on to Crete two days later. I would meet my buyer in Crete if he showed up. Tyrants were notoriously unreliable. But that was ok. I got my revenge on them in the final price with a twenty grand penalty for every day they made me wait, the bastards. And this guy I would be meeting was a true tyrant. A Nigerian prince, he told me, and it checked out. But his royal blood didn't change the fact that he was a cretin, always late and with a taste for sadism as an added bonus. He was a small-time player with a big checking account and an even bigger mouth. I would have to find a way to keep Silibi out of range of his foolishness. He'd shoot off his mouth and spoil everything.

I knew I should have come alone, but as I grew older, I began to hate being alone. I'd become a lonely arms dealer who likes to cuddle at night. Is there a problem with that?

We got back on my rented bike and sped off into the valley. Silibi's goal was less than two clicks away as the crow flies, but it would take us an hour to get there along the narrow streets, cobbled switchbacks, and slow traffic. I would be needing another drink by the time we arrived.

Athens was fine. Great street life. Great food. Our days in Santorini went too fast. Silibi had never been before so everything was new and I got to play tour guide. It is a marvelous place even for a cynical bastard like me. We visited the various colored beaches and found the best viewpoints to drink wine and toast to my age and to her success. I would have preferred to return to a favorite island of mine, the island of *Kefalonia* for the great wines there, instead of Santorini, but it was too far out of the way and I promised Silibi we'd do it next trip. I found I was continually holding out carrots to Silibi for future travel adventures. In the back of my mind, I was convinced she would tire of me before long. So, nothing lost. It was unlikely I would have to deliver on all my promises.

Silibi said she would like to go to Symi too next time because she'd heard it was the best island for couples. 'What, so we're a couple now?' I cracked. She punched me in the arm, and for a minute I thought how it might be nice to be a couple, commit to each other, and maybe have a kid or a dog or something. Then I thought better. Bad guys make shit husbands and worse fathers. I would probably last until the first diaper change and then admit that I had made a mistake. Silibi didn't deserve that.

I chose Crete as the location to meet my client. It wasn't one of my favorite islands, though the food was better there than most. It was a big island, more room to stretch, and it offered the possibility of getting lost if somehow a deal went sour. The other rocks in the neighborhood were so small that you couldn't fart without making the papers. I wanted space to maneuver and some anonymity if I could get it. If it all went well and quickly enough I might just surprise Silibi and take her to Symi to get that coupling out of her system.

It would feel good to have this bit of business behind me, and I began playing mental tapes of my previous encounters with my client.

All my clients were shits, but most had the social skills to keep their worst qualities hidden from view. Not so with Prince Nbuko. He went by Daryl, actually. The 'Prince' moniker was my doing, though he claimed to be a prince from the Igbo tribe. No prince of a guy, however.

We had some troubles in the past, but the money was too good I had been unable to walk away from him. He eventually paid and paid well, complete with penalties for infractions and late arrivals. But doing business with him was always messy, always stressful, and always unpleasant for anyone who happened to be in the area at the time. Despite my warnings, he showed up for our meetings with some new friend. I hated that. I wouldn't put up with it for any other client. And then he beat up two paid female companions the last time we were out– one very badly – and if I hadn't intervened, she would have been found floating face down in the Seine. I appealed to his reason and told him to kill his own Nigerian ladies if he had something to prove to the world, and leave the lovely French ones whom I had procured for him alone. He laughed and let them go, but I didn't appreciate the woman's blood on my shirtsleeves and shoe bottoms. And there was always some cousin or nephew he brought along to impress who was wide-eyed and stupid so that I felt like a babysitter for juvenile delinquents more than a dealer of arms.

I now carried a concealed weapon when I met with Prince Daryl, a little .38 Smith and Wesson Special. This I had never done before because my deals were typically civilized and controlled. Feeling now that anything could happen, I'd be damned if it would be me sitting there unarmed and unnerved by some wise guy with big ambitions and loose morals. My job wasn't easy in the best of times, but I knew I couldn't expect my clients to act like Christian choirboys when it came to buying weapons of mass destruction. I got into the business on a whim and it was my honest face that helped me convince my clients to push the send button on a wire transfer sometimes a full twelve weeks before the goods were delivered to some dirty warehouse in the middle of Bumfuck, Egypt.

Silibi's presence was making me nervous these past few days, as she was suddenly getting all lovey-dovey, which was not like her. I was going to need four hours alone, with her both absent from the scene and unaware of my whereabouts. That was without the event of a snafu brought about by the Prince or his companion *du jour* when our deal went down.

I'd figured out a plan.

I scheduled my bike for a visit to the shop to get a tune-up. It didn't need repair, but I could use a weak handbrake as an excuse to get away from Silibi. When we arrived in Crete, I alerted her to the fact that I would have to get the bike serviced during the afternoon of the following day,

As I slipped away, I had time to think. I hoped this would be my last deal. If I could upsell the Prince by another million or two, I could come away with plenty to keep me warm and in wine for as long as my ticker kept ticking.

It was unbelievable how the armament game works. It's a monster business of 70 Billion a year, yet almost a total secret. It gets very little press and don't ask me why. The primary players come out of governments of France, Russia, Belgium, and Germany, but the vast percentage comes from 'my country 'tis of thee,' sweet land of the USA. In 2011 the US accounted for 70% of the market, but that number has dropped off some. Lockheed Martin, Raytheon, and General Dynamics are the most effective and successful Merchants of Death, and if you have doubts, just ask yourself, 'who armed Saddam?'

Volatility in the Middle East and Asia are the growth areas for the foreseeable future. The goal is to stay at war or on the verge of it. And in America, who sells guns? The president on down, together with military attachés, embassy staff, ambassadors, and probably the cleaning lady, all acting as sales reps for the arms industry. The bureaucracy that keeps the engine running is the Defense Security Cooperation Agency, collecting a 3.5% surcharge on all the deals it negotiates. Obama has sold more weaponry than any administration since WWII. Spots like Ukraine, Crimea, and the South China Sea ring the alarm bells and provide the demand for new business.

How can I not try to get a piece of this? I make anywhere from 30 to 40% on any sale, from a case of assault rifles to a container of cluster bombs. It is a shame I have no F-35 fighter aircraft in my pocket to sell; one plane would keep me in green through the next several wars and generations.

And Silibi, what had gotten into her? Suddenly she was so sweet and affectionate. It was beginning to look like love and that was far scarier than doing a deal with my rogue Igbo prince. In normal times I would have simply abandoned her somewhere – leave her enough money to get home – but nothing more. No calls, no goodbyes, and no forwarding address.

This time I had to say I was intrigued. I liked the attention. I liked her. She was everything any man could want and I no longer had the feeling she was just in it for the free ride that came with being my companion.

I dropped off the bike and planned to return before the close of business. Then I headed up the steep hillside to the little bar where I was set to meet my own sugar daddy. Prince Daryl. He was at the dartboard back in the dark part of the bar, a drink in one hand and an unattractive Greek barfly on the other. He was teaching her the sport and had his hands all over her showing how to stand, aim, and release. She looked like a few more throws and she would be ready to play from a horizontal position.

'What is new, my brother?' asked Daryl.

'Hello, my friend. How is everything? How is your family?' It was a mild dig - though as I expected- my meaning was lost to him.

"I am fine, very fine as you can see. This lady is keeping me company and learning the business of dart throwing, which as you know is something I do very well. I learned to play in college in London when I studied there many years ago. Look at her throw. What a specimen, no?'

The girl threw the dart which landed sidewise on the board and bounced off to the floor. She found this hysterical and collapsed into Daryl's arms. He used the opportunity to grab her ample bottom and looked at me like a cat playing with a captured mouse, proud of his catch.

'Yes, I see you have kept your skills,' I said. 'It's a marvelous game to be sure.'

'Why not get yourself a beverage and then we can sit and talk about business. Are you ready to do business?' he asked.

'It is why I'm here, my friend,' I said. I went to the bar and a man covered in coarse black hair served me a whiskey on the rocks in a cloudy highball glass.

'Or perhaps you would rather I ask Natasha here if she has a pretty friend for you, eh?'

'Oh, that won't be necessary,' I assured him. I thought of Silibi back at the hotel pool and wished immediately that I was there with her. My full whiskey glass was not enough to discourage Daryl from buying shots to accompany it.

I drank my ouzo and Prince Daryl drank three. Finally, we left the bar for his limo parked outside, or so he claimed. Fortunately, Natasha had passed out and he left her snoring in a booth.

The limo turned out to be a clown car of sorts. It was hidden in back so I did not see it when I entered the bar. A young man stood beside it, dressed as a chauffeur. Daryl said it was his cousin Clyde.

The car was an old fiat pick-up that some automotive butcher had converted into a stretch limousine of sorts. The door squeaked on its rusty hinges as his driver opened it. Leaning in, his jacket fell slightly open to reveal the handle of a pistol and a holster strap beneath his stained green livery. I knew weapons; it was a Sig Sauer P220 Compact. I had no fear that he planned to kill me, but did feel some trepidation that he might accidentally shoot us or himself. This was Prince Daryl's new surprise, a limo driver, a cousin, armed and dangerous.

The interior of the limo was more laughable still, though I dared not show my amusement. He might order Cousin Clyde to take me out for a joy ride. But it took all my self-control to maintain a business continence in the face of the bar, fully outfitted with plastic Champaign glasses, three bottles of cheap booze, and an early model tape deck playing Donna Summers. I could only hope that Clyde wouldn't hit a switch for a disco ball.

'So what do you have for me, my friend?' asked Daryl.

I was prepared for this; after several exchanges over secure webmail discussing items and costs and full details for each and every weapon, it was like he had shaken the etch-a-sketch so we could begin again. He did this each time. He wanted my friendly discount.

'You read my messages, Prince. I know you did because you replied.'

'Yes, oh that, of course, but I am your friend so you must offer me something special.' he said. I cringed waiting for a friendly slug in the shoulder, but it didn't come.

'I am prepared to ship everything you asked for, as agreed. Prices, as agreed. I will toss in an extra case of the assault rifles for free once payment is confirmed.

'Three cases, you say?'

'Two cases. No more Daryl. This is business, friends, or no friends. I have to eat.' I could play the game as well.

'Ah, you are so cheap with me. Next time I will expect a very special discount. And I will want some of those 50 caliber machine guns to mount on Toyota pick-up trucks. You can do a lot of damage with those big guns. I have seen it. I saw it in Mogadishu. It was great to watch. These guns, cousin, they don't just kill; they vaporize the bodies of the enemy. Like watermelons.'

Clyde looked back from the front seat and smiled. He would have preferred to be driving a Toyota pick-up with a mounted 50-caliber. I could see it in his eyes.

Again I thought of Silibi, my smart, sophisticated Silibi, floating on a raft back at the hotel pool. She would be ashamed to know that I was here in the space sharing time with two sociopaths.

A car pulled into the parking lot and three men got out. They looked tough, but paid no attention to us, although I thought I saw one man glance at our Rube Goldberg Limo and giggle.

'Drive, cousin. Let's get out of here.'

This I did not want.

'They mean nothing, Prince, I protested. 'They are just going inside for a drink.'

'I did not like their looks, those men. Just drive, cousin. We will complete our business on the move.'

I thought we had completed our business. But I again anticipated Daryl's next move.

'A drink then, shall we? To seal the deal.' he said.

'Fine, Daryl, after your down payment I will be pleased to have a drink. I will greenlight the shipment immediately when I get back to my hotel. And you can wire the balance as we agreed.'

'Do we have a deal?' I asked, pushing to close.

'With three extra cases of semi-automatic rifles,' he said as he poured three shots of ouzo.

'Two.' I insisted.

'Ah, you are so cheap with me! Yes, two cases. And all the rest. As agreed.' He handed me the glass and reached to pass one to Clyde, then held it to his lips.

'The down-payment, Prince?'

'Oh yes, I have forgotten. Here it is.' He reached into his pocket. If something were to go south, it would be now. But the wads of dirty hundred dollar bills emerged from his jacket packets, one after the other. He had managed to conceal fifty thousand in the pockets of his suit. There it was, and it looked legitimate. I would count and confirm back at the hotel.

We drank.

When the shots were duly tossed, I looked to Cousin Clyde. 'Take me to the bike shop at the bottom of the hill,' I instructed Cousin Clyde. 'I can manage myself from there.'

With a destination in mind, Clyde pressed the accelerator and we started bouncing down the cobblestones. A limo in Crete was like the proverbial bull in the china shop, and this limo ran on worn-out light pick-up suspension. A bull ride would have been smoother.

'Slow down,' I suggested, but Clyde pressed on as Daryl poured three more ouzos, spilling most of it on the floor and the seat. Just ahead, a car turned towards us from a side street and Clyde swerved left and ran up on the boulevard. We bottomed out with the screech of metal on stone. The rear wheels spun free in the air as the ass end of the limo was lifted off the cobbles. We had run aground.

One look at the situation, the neighborhood, the gang of young boys casually approaching, and I could see it was time to be off.

'I'm going to walk, Prince. Thanks for everything.' I opened the squeaky door and began walking down the hill as the two of them emerged from the car to assess the damages. The car rocked like a see-saw balancing on the high curb. The wheel guard was smashed in, and the car looked like a comical carnival ride. I nearly laughed again but kept it to myself as best I could. From the corner of my eye, it looked like Clyde opened his coat and touched the handle of the pistol under his arm. There must be something he could shoot, I imagined him thinking.

I was five minutes' walk from the bike shop, and I couldn't get there fast enough. The bike was fine, breaks adjusted almost unnecessarily, and I hopped on and headed home. Silibi was showering when I arrived, so I locked the cash in the wall safe, changed my shirt, and was ready to go when she appeared, fresh and lovely.

'Something to eat?' I suggested.

'I'm starving,' she said and came into my arms.

'Let's go,' I said.

What's wrong,' she asked?' You look upset.'

'I'm fine', I said. 'Fine now. I'm with you.'

She seemed to like that and held me tight as she rode behind me through the streets of Crete. I wished to head far away from Daryl but had to return to near where I had bailed from the unlucky limo to catch the main road out of town.

The breeze felt wonderful, and Silibi's arms around me felt even better. I felt dirty from my business dealings but promised myself it would be the end of it. I would find some other way to make a living if one day the money ran out. Maybe be a husband. A dad-

I heard a pop and thought a tire blew but felt no wobble. In a moment I did feel something strange. It had nothing to do with the bike. It was Silibi. Her embrace had gone limp.

I slowed and only just managed to catch her before she fell.

'What is it?' I asked. 'What's happened to you?'

Her eyes were closed. She looked like she was sleeping. I looked at her frantically, pulling back an eyelid and seeing that her pupil did not respond to the light. Nothing. No sign of blood. No sign of illness. I took her head in my hands and spoke into her face. 'What is it, Sil? What's happened?' She remained painfully still, but I sense a fleeting motion ahead. I glanced up the road to see a teenage boy throw something into the bushes and run. I lay Silibi flat on the roadside gravel, and as I took my hands away from her hair, I felt a wet dampness and saw red. Blood. I fought her hair away and found its source. At the back of her head, there was a small penetration, with her life dripping from it.

I went back later to the scene of the crime. From where I had put the bike down, I walked up the hill to see where the boy had been, where he threw something and ran. In the weeds, I found the gun. It was Cousin Clyde's, the Sig Sauer. One bullet was missing from the clip. One was still in the chamber.

Silibi was dead. She had family, though I had never met them. Could I ship her body home? Abandon her here? I was overcome with sadness and shame.

Tomorrow was my 59th birthday. The Tarot Card Reader had been wrong. Or was she? My .38 Special felt heavy in my pocket.

CLIFF WILLIAMSON

"TAILS"

SELECTION FROM SHINING NEW TESTAMENT, BOOK OF BEAUTY

> Dr. Harry Wong's genetic genius conquered Fall Fashion Week in a single stroke, unmatched since Yves St. Laurent put the first black model on a runway.
>
> Our **Gene Watch** Correspondent was there and survived to tell us about it.
>
> — DATELINE NEW YORK, SEPTEMBER 2027
> EXCLUSIVE

The spectacle at Tails Club on West 62nd began before the crowd took their seats. Extreme security would have dampened the mood were it not that even the security contingent consisted of Harry Wong copyrights, bulging with bionic features and implanted with techno gizmos. Every model arrived on one of Wong's private jets direct from *Agenzia del Modello* of Milan or *Clinique Génétique* of Marseilles. They were secured from public access like secret weapons.

Receptionists and escorts displayed the effects of gene massage in their faces, hair, and skin. Models of indeterminate gender served *tofushi* and *piscola*, and bore pates free of hair except for sculpted eyebrow 'rings' perfectly circumnavigating their craniums. My reaction was abhorrence until I recalled how three years earlier, I'd written off the long-legged BarbieGirls™ as busty barbarians on stilts. Now I am married to two of them.

Circulating among the masses were WideEyes™ Third Generation, with corneas of bright pastel and eyelids carpeted in natural fur. There were MitChins™, clefts embedded with gemstones. Models were naked but for accent tatts and body paints in the Wong tradition. Genitalia and fleshy nooks were outfitted with every manner of piercing by ChainLinx®, a loyal Wong collaborator since pre-lib days. Studs, rings, implants, and accessories featured lapis lazuli and chrysalis, trademarks of the good doctor.

Wong unleashed his WFD (weapons of fashion destruction) for maximum effect. Every few minutes he triggered a bigger more beautiful bomb, each a direct hit on the crowd's imagination. Out came the Duplicate™ line, reaching a new apotheosis of authenticity, featuring celebrities from the great movies of the 1940s to a present-day mix of heroes and villains. A perfect parody of President-elect Veras drew bawdy laughter as she danced a perverse jig, twisting into impossible poses.

Materializing on stage were the improved SpinalCoiffeurs™, engineered with remarkable hair, thicker and silkier than earlier efforts. Wong capitalized on a method which starts hair growth quicker, without the coarseness and lower follicle density produced by accelerated growth hormone. The new spinal hair looked natural, beginning at the crease of the buttocks and rising to the nape.

When Wong finally shuffled on stage, his high pitched voice called to his freaky friends, the men, the women, and those who defy categorization. "I bring you what has never been seen except by my most intimate staff. This culmination of my life's work has succeeded beyond my wildest dreams, and you know my dreams are wild." The crowd roared. "I now share my achievement with you. Welcome my latest line, my most beautiful creatures. I bring you Tails™ 2027."

The lights came up to reveal a display which will impact aesthetic surgery, genetic manipulation, and the world of fashion forever. *The resurrection of the human tail.*

A dozen men and women stood before me with tails of cartilage, flesh, and silky hair. Varying in length from a few inches to a foot and a half, they sprouted just above the ass like a natural continuation of the spinal cord. The effect was stunning, primal, transporting me back to my genetic past, to a full recovery of that which was thought forever lost. Seeing those tails made me feel like a marvelous animal, proud and virile. I was aroused by the very sight. It was beautiful. It was sensual. And *I wanted one!*

Mayhem ensued. Hundreds swarmed the stage, endangering the models as they stood like deer in the footlights. Wong's bouncers, bred for situations like these, retook control and escorted the creatures backstage.

The crowd was euphoric. Wong touched on something we mortals had never understood. We all wanted tails. We just didn't know it. I followed Wong's menagerie backstage, where the mods huddled together. For seven years, the tailed ones were isolated but for Wong and a few staff. I shouted my compliments. "Brilliant! Beautiful!" I kissed every mod within reach. They began to smile, and - I kid you not! - *hold each other by the tail.*

I reached for the appendage of the closest mod, whose name I learned was Rhea, an orphan from Bombay now adopted by Wong. She was gorgeous. She reacted with a start when I touched her member covered in a silky fur that matched her pubis. She pulled back, but as her fears dissipated, she permitted me to complete the caress. For her, it was novel. For me, nirvana.

Tail touching was an icebreaking leap across a taxonomic gap.

These creatures were in a class apart, nearly another species. Yet Rhea's sharing of her tail with me merged us back together again into one happy genetic family.

Wong noticed me. I jumped to introduce myself. "Cliff Williamson of <u>Argentine Independent Magazine</u>. Dr. Wong, you've done it again. No. You've done something brand new, a most wonderful thing indeed!"

"So you like it then," he said in his high squeak. His eyes showed a glint of pleasure. "Good. I'm glad you like my creatures. But I fear you must go. They are exhausted. This was an emotional experience. They have heightened sensitivity, a depth of feeling beyond the norm. It's beautiful but works against them if stressed or tired. They die at the drop of a hat, poor darlings!"

"An appointment then, Dr. Wong. Tomorrow?"

"We will talk. Call in a week."

He's not taken my calls, and meanwhile, I dream of tails. Wong stretched my definition of beauty like a cervix. I feel like an illiterate villager staring in awe at the Renaissance cathedral as it takes shape, while Wong the Builder shouts to us all, "Bring stones! I need more stones!"

MAN OVERBOARD

I was surprised to see the open and empty elevator on the ground floor, awaiting me like an open tomb, on a Friday at 11 PM in one of the busiest buildings in a city known for its nightlife, where a penthouse bar inaugurated only 3 months earlier had been rocking the city's social pages as 'the place to see and be seen.'

I stepped in and pushed the button for the 42nd floor. The door slid closed and the Carpenters sang their classic "I'm Up On Top Of The World." I smirked at the irony.

Poor Karen. A beautiful talented successful young woman at the peak of her professional career had starved herself to death in a haze of anorexia. I, on the other hand, was full and fat from my business dinner with Craig Mission, the star entrepreneur of the city and the times. I had three martinis and felt each one. Craig had six that evaporated into his mouth like water. I had to either learn how to drink or learn how to stop drinking. I was a short hitter, but we'd signed our deal.

As the elevator sped upwards, my body shivered and shook, not due to the night airs but to the nervous energy I carried within me.

'Why was I doing this?' I asked myself while knowing full well that I had no choice in the matter. I was a man, and my manly hackles had been raised, my ego stroked, my id craving nourishment. My reptilian brain could not refuse this encounter any more than I could say no to a glass of ice water at the gates of a desert oasis.

The elevator slowed suddenly like a pop fly reaching its apex. My stomach continued to rise about two inches further than the rest of my body. As it stopped, the door opened to the entrance of the rooftop bar. The lights were low, and I stood still to let my eyes adjust. The receptionist stand stood abandoned. As the elevator door closed, Karen Carpenter gave way to the throbbing heartbeat of some unnamed Ibiza House playlist. The rhythm restarted my own flow of life-giving blood to my arteries and capillaries. And hopefully diverted some much-needed oxygen to my brain.

The restaurant was empty. So was the bar. There was no sign of humanity save a glass of champagne positioned in the center of a cocktail napkin in the middle of the bar. Written in lipstick on the napkin were the words, 'Yes! For you!'

I took it. The liquid was ice cold and sweet.

I moved towards the outdoor deck. There was a lone figure standing there. A woman dressed in white silk, hair up in a braided coil, shoes like tiny clouds, a soft breeze blowing. With her eyes, she seemed to be feasting on the cityscape below. She too held a glass of champagne. She turned slightly towards me. She wore a large green emerald on a golden chain around her slim neck.

I should not have come. I had seduced this woman and now it was her setting the trap for me. But her presence drew me closer as if by some irresistible force of gravitation. I was close enough to see her eyes now, green like emeralds, with a deep spark of light at the core of each.

'Hello,' she said, turning back to feast further on the city. I placed my hand on the rail beside hers, which she then covered with her own. Her touch was light as a macaroon, yet it held me in place like an animal snared in a trap.

'Where is everyone?' I asked.

'Everyone is here who needs to be here,' she replied. 'Are you pleased to see me?'

'Why, yes, of course, I…, to be honest, I'm a little…. I'm a-'

'Shhhhh!' she whispered. 'There is no need to speak, is there?' she asked. She put a finger to my lips. 'Not yet at least.'

She put her glass on the rail, then took mine from my hand and placed it beside hers. She faced me.

'There!' she said. 'Now you have my full attention.' She stroked my lapels. 'Do I have yours?'

I tried to raise my arms, but I was paralyzed. She could have pitched me over the side if she had wished it. I was helpless.

She leaned into me and placed a knee softly between my thighs. She reached behind me and stroked my neck with one hand while caressing my lips with her other.

I let out a small moan, completely involuntarily, and she smiled at the sound.

'Aw, poor man!' She purred. 'You're frightened by me, aren't you? There's no need to be frightened.'

She tilted her face to mine, moved her lips close to my lips, and opened wide.

In terror, I saw her sharp pointed teeth gleam in the moonlight.

EIGHT

Searing gobs of radioactive goo dribbled from the reactors, burning holes through the floor of the containment vessels. The superheated water gushed to the once calm sea, converting it in seconds to a bubbling maelstrom. Creatures swimming in the shallows were boiled alive.

A reef a hundred meters offshore from the radioactive water's entry once swarmed with life. Even now – compared to surrounding waters – it was a showplace of diversity. There an octopus lay dying. A cancerous tumor despoiled his soft underbelly. He hid in a cove, sheltering beneath a protrusion of corral, awaiting imminent death. Highly sensitive to pain, he felt the unmistakable rise in temperature and moved quickly to escape it, heading further out to sea. As he propelled himself forward, the surge washed over him. As if inhaling hot tar, his lungs filled with radioactive liquid. He stretched out eight arms in radial agony and settled into a deep hole where cooler water collected in a hollow pillar. He lay corpse-like, unable to hunt, swim, or eat for six days.

The Giant Pacific Octopus had no real business off the coast of Japan, so close to shore in that part of the sea. He had come as a stowaway on a commercial fishing boat from Malaysia, a thousand nautical miles. Despite his near collapse, lying on his back and vulnerable to any passing predator, his thirst for world travel had not ended. Not even close.

The octopus awoke to good news and bad. The good news? Radiation exposure – a frequent cause of cancer - cured it this time instead. The 4-year-old cephalopod's tumor changed from fatal to benign overnight.

The bad news? Two of his eight appendages were bitten off and pilfered by a passing sleeper shark. He would need to survive six weeks of vulnerability while his arms regenerated. If lucky, they would grow back stronger than before. Like so much, it depended on diet and exercise. He felt hunger, and food was at hand. He gathered a pile of small octopuses, dead or dying, strewn across the seafloor. They too had been in the path of contaminated water. They tasted rank. His mouth was scorched, and his ultra-sensitive suction cups forming two rows the length of each of his remaining arms were red and raw. He had survived a fight for life. Nature and danger are synonymous, ever more so when stirred into nuclear bathwater.

The Pacific Giant ate but searched for better nourishment. He constantly sought better, even in the best of times. In the struggle to swim with two missing arms, jet propulsion provided motion, squirting water behind as his arms and occasional pumping motions of his main body provided directional control.

He could swim for short periods at speeds of twenty-four kilometers per hour. He couldn't reach top speed in his debilitated condition, but a southern current nudged him forward. He swam, drifted, and nibbled for days and for two-hundred kilometers to Choshi Port to the rich kelp beds where marine life was abundant. His new limbs budded but would be useless in a fight with all but the weakest adversaries. A sea otter or another octopus would be his most likely antagonist. His species wasn't known for friendliness, and he expected no quarter from a member of his tribe. He led a lonely life and preferred it so.

When he reached the coastline of Chiba, the kelp beds overflowed with whelks, clams, and crabs to restore his health and promote regeneration. His other limbs were two meters long. The nubs were one-tenth their normal size, but they had made a good start, and each day grew longer and stronger.

He found a knoll covered with sand and coral, some stones and pieces of waterlogged encrusted lumber, offering protective cover for hiding and hunting. He was a true predator, full of tricks and decoys to lure prey close and then pounce for the kill. He could distract a shrimp with the tip of one arm while encircling from behind with another. He could reach out and grab. He could form a cloak and drop suddenly from above. Watching him hunt was trying; it was over before one knew where to look.

Even more deadly was his ability to hide by changing colors and manipulating his shape. Most creatures would pass within centimeters unaware that something was stalking in the shadows.

Though often alone and cantankerous, quick to fight, and with few social skills, octopuses do – at least once in their lifetime – reach out and touch someone to assure propagation of the species.

There was a female in the neighborhood who seemed willing enough. She was a beauty, not a Giant Pacific but close, and while she demonstrated no outward sign of encouragement, female octopuses rarely do. She at least had not yet tried to strangle and eat him. It might be love.

As his new arms grew functional, he began feeling the changes that come over an octopus preparing to mate. Sex was no rush job. Truly, the risk of cannibalism from the female was without a doubt his greatest danger. Many octopuses mated from a distance, sneaking up and attempting to pass along packets of sperm, placing them at arms' length in the female's body. Sometimes, if there was a mutual good feeling, the male might risk an intimate act of affection, covering the female with its body, and interacting face-to-face, not unlike making out. It all depended on the female's disposition. Even after a great session of cephalopod lovemaking, the male might end up strangled and dragged into the female's lair to be consumed at leisure.

The Great Pacific male was patient and took the time necessary for his two limbs to fully regenerate so he could flee if attacked, fight if provoked, and perform if allowed as the mating ritual unfolded. When the day finally arrived, he came knocking.

He extended his long and specially equipped arm to the right of his head, and it stiffened. The female showed no sign of interest, but made no move to scoot away either, and committed no act of aggression against him. So far so good.

He inched closer. He was going for full coital contact and had already moved some sperm packets into the tip of his hectocotylus, the third right arm. As he approached, he extended this penis arm towards the female to pass a sperm packet like a relay baton into a crevice beneath her mantle. She would store it there until ready to fertilize her eggs.

He pulled her close and she came willingly, arms entwining and bodies clinging in embrace. If nothing bad happened, this pose could last four hours. It went so much better than it might have. To think that sometimes a male is left with no other option than to tear off his penis arm and present it to the female, hoping she'll use it for her pleasure without killing him.

He weighed 70 kilos; she weighed slightly more. As they frolicked, the sand billowed into clouds and they danced themselves into a tight bundle.

Had they completed the act, both he and his female companion would die within weeks, starved and emaciated; the life of an octopus lasts for only one such entanglement. Fertilized eggs would be affixed to hard surfaces, hatching within a month, and protected by watchful parents. Both adults would stop eating and die of starvation.

Not this time. The barbed spear broke the surface, penetrating the female from above, a direct hit between her eyes, piercing one of her three hearts. Snatched from his arms, she was drawn up into a skiff above.

A shocking and unexpected act of *coitus interruptus* had saved the Great Pacific male's life, allowing him to live long, and – some might say - prosper.

Though uninjured, the male was traumatized. As his chosen mate disappeared above him, he fled to his safe space, blending in with protective coloration and shape-shifting to match surrounding corrals on the seafloor. He lay motionless, frightened but stoic. He had escaped death again. A bit of black ink – the last vestige of his dying lover – swirled past him with a hint of pheromone-laden odor caressing his sensory glands, a tragic final kiss goodbye.

The octopus was hyper-alert. He saw polarized light, distinguished color, heard, smelled, felt, and tasted. The most intelligent of invertebrates, he held the highest brain-to-body mass ratio of them all, greater than many vertebrates. Only part of his nervous system could fit into his brain; two-thirds of his neurons honeycombed the nerve cords of his arms, and those arms acted independently from his brain. His brain was the server; his arms were semi-autonomous.

The octopus was not consciously aware that – without the fisherman's disruption– consummating the sex act would have soon killed both him and his mate. He knew he had made a narrow escape. If one didn't count the loss of several thousand potential offspring, he was lucky once again.

He lay motionless until hunger dragged him back to life. He ventured outside the cave, moved through the current, and nibbled scallops, which further sparked his appetite. He grazed on a bed of abalone until dawn.

The vibrations of a trawler passing overhead stirred him alert. He had stowed away once before on a fishing boat and had vague memories of slithering into a hatch where he feasted on crab. Impulsively he decided to hitch another ride. As the boat sputtered past, he reached up with one long arm and latched on, pulled himself into a protected niche in a recess near the propeller, and headed east.

The ship was the "Nisshin Maru," a 2000-ton whaling factory refitted for scientific research, a crew of three with a team of fifteen scientists aboard gathering data on Pacific Ocean pollution. Setting sail from Yokohama, they set up equipment in their labs and stowed personal gear in their cabins. While they worked, the octopus pillaged, pulling himself up over the rail at night and sliding along the decks and storage areas. The food locker was a disappointment. Most of the food was pre-packaged, but he stuck with the cruise, knowing he could abandon ship at any time in case of danger, discomfort, or lack of food. He watched from dark corners as the Asian scientists, oceanographers, marine biologists, and chemists scurried to and fro, concentrating on their mission.

Awarded a research grant from the University of Tokyo, their itinerary included stops in the waters near Fukushima, then onward to The Great Pacific Garbage Patch. Their final destination was Long Beach where they'd link up with student statisticians from UCLA and Stanford for an on-shore collaboration to crunch data and report results.

The stow-away remained hidden overboard or behind a refrigerator with a large pan of water beneath it, keeping hydrated during the long days. He hunted food and opportunities at night. He was never content to eat and sleep. He was curious, adventurous, and confident in his abilities to escape danger or observation.

Night's shadowy darkness was perfect for exploration. When the vessel was in motion, he dropped over the side, slithered down the metal body of the ship, held on to a fastening cleat with four arms, and fished for edibles with the four others. Creatures often affixed themselves to the sides of the ship, and he made quick work to remove their shells and eat their tasty guts. There were also leftovers of the meals from the crew. They kept a tidy ship and refused to throw refuse into the sea. Their garbage provided spicy titbits.

One night he was captured by one of the crew. Her name was Ichica, the IT Specialist. A dedicated geek, her dream was to interface technology with non-human subjects. She loved the Football World Cup and nursed the idea of developing the next Oracle, a more credible predictor than the clairvoyant cats, pigs, or Paul the Octopus of 2014.

On the night of his incarceration, the Great Pacific Octopus was pursuing richer sources of protein inside the laboratory. A delicious smell wafted under the door. As long as there was a hole big enough to insert his beak, he could push his entire body through. That was Plan A.

Most of his body had passed under the door when he felt a tug on the last three of his arms, gripping tight as a predator's teeth. As his mantle and major organs had already passed beneath the door, he couldn't effectively squirt ink into the eyes of his captor. Still, he was certain he could wrestle free with brute force and a dash of slime. He would scurry for the first sign of cover the moment he made his break. He was not prepared for the strong hands which followed him like shadows, grasped him firmly by the body, and tossed him into a large seawater aquarium.

A lid slammed down and he was alone inside a glass box with stainless steel roof and rocky bottom. An air pump injected bubbles into the saltwater. With only a blurred image of his captor through the glass in a dimly lighted room, he spent the night alone, and on the morning of the next day, his true education began.

Ichica was attentive, bringing fresh scallops and broad leaves of fresh kelp. She stared through the glass for hours and stood accompanied by another unattractive human who stared with her. The octopus had experienced these creatures before, never pleasantly, and was determined to escape at the first opportunity.

Since the voyage began, Ichica had been working after hours, constructing an interface which utilized stimuli from a living creature to generate coded output. She had been eager to have a go with an octopus and see if the rumors of 'the intelligent cephalopod' were true. Besides, an octopus has dexterity. A chicken could peck three times on the red button, receive a grain of corn, and be a hero. A monkey could touch red, blue, and white buttons in proper sequence, a bell would ring and a piece of banana would drop into his dish as if by god. But an octopus was quite capable to perform varied and complex tasks. If Ichica could find a clever way for an octopus to express himself, she could attract attention.

Predicting game-winners in the World Cup was an obvious ruse. Not even the smartest football expert could make predictions with more than 65% accuracy – hardly better than "flip of a coin" odds. But if the effects of animal input and an amusing gismo could be combined, it could mean money, notoriety, and a boost to the cause of getting humans to respect their fellow species in the shared habitation of the earth. For now, she would concentrate on a simple release of food, and once basic coded learning was established, she would work to assemble something more sophisticated.

That – at least – was her idea. What Ichica did not expect was that her Guinea Pig – or Guinea Puss – would be such a quick study and an amazingly cooperative subject.

The scallop treats elicited great loyalty -almost love- between subject and scientist. The octopus curled around her hand, caressed it and came close to what might be described as an embrace. Ichica was amazed and amused, and the relationship of octopus to captor grew to become an engaging curiosity aboard ship.

She named him "EIGHT" and before long he was sitting in a shallow cake pan filled halfway with seawater in a privileged position on her desk while Ichica input her daily readouts. EIGHT took an interest in everything Ichica did, watching carefully, touching what Ichica touched, and positioning himself in the best position to see Ichica perform. The computer – a large screen MacBook – held a particular fascination, and sometimes Ichica had to scold the cephalopod to prevent him from climbing atop the keyboard and interfering with her work.

One afternoon when the Nisshin Maru drifted in the middle of The Pacific Gyre, Ichica was called away from her work station. She left a video playing on her computer. For the benefit of Eight, she chose, "The Life of the Giant Pacific Octopus." When she returned three hours later, the video on her computer had run its course, and the screen reverted to a file displaying her data. Typed across the page was some gibberish, typical of previous occasions when Eight parked himself on the edge of her keyboard.

eqdwdqdfqwweqrewwqrwretjdadrtoiqertoérp3q4trtjhwrtj ´qegefyu9wer9ewr9gewrgy9er9er78q80ewr67sdfhreqtuarer8t5ty-ereyuryuertheriutertertuerterthweurt…

Nothing of interest. But then, two blank lines appeared, along with something quite different.

1234567890888888888888888888888888888888888

Ichica could only imagine that someone was toying with her.

She looked for EIGHT but he was AWOL. She gave notice to her colleagues and asked them to search. Nothing. He was gone.

Eight – it was later surmised - had gone overboard to explore on his own the plastic playground of the Great Pacific Gyre. Two times the size of Texas, three times the size of France, the Gyre was an island of floating plastic garbage. Nearly the combined weight of every sea creature living in the oceans, plastic waste would soon overtake and strangle all sea life in the entire oceanic world. Besides being the subject of study of Ichica and her team on the Nisshin Maru, it was now the subject as well for a close investigation by EIGHT, the newly literate octopus. The gyre held everything imaginable that floated. Much of it was lost fishing gear, lines and ropes and floats, and discarded lifejackets. But there were 800 million tons, much of it broken down into tiny flecks of plastic with 500 years remaining until decomposition. Coincidentally, the gyre was a floating pharmacy. Massive quantities of prescription drugs were released into the world and discarded when illness had run its course. The drugs not fully consumed went out with the trash and ended up floating in rivers, lakes, and oceans.

An octopus can open a jar better than grandpa's weathered hands, and EIGHT was having a field day opening medicine bottles, swallowing their contents, and riding out the often hallucinogenic trips which resulted, clinging to a child's floatie, a weather buoy, a Styrofoam cooler, or a fend-off. He developed a fondness for Ecstasy. He had good trips and bad, mind-expanding, and terrifying, but before long became sick, not from his drug habit but from the microscopic plastic bits that filled his stomach.

EIGHT struggled back to the Nisshin Maru, and with all remaining strength pulled himself over the side, where he collapsed and was found by the ship's cat, and rescued by Ichica in the nick of time.

EIGHT was unable to eat solid food for a week but Ichica managed so get some broth past his beak so that he became a functioning cephalopod once again. In another week Ichica was ready to risk restoring to EIGHT the right to sit at his privileged place in the pan of seawater on her desk.

EIGHT's long arms soon began exploring the keys of her computer. Ichica sat with her cup of tea entering data when she felt before she saw a tentacle pass behind her chair, reaching around her to the space bar of her keyboard. She watched EIGHT composed a new message.

'Space, space, space, 8.

Space, space, space, ?'

The end of the tentacle now went from the keyboard to Ithaca's wrist, where it wrapped around and tapped three times.

Ichica sat in silence. Crazy. Absurd. Oh, what the hell. She entered,

'Space, space, space. I C H I C A.'

EIGHT moved closer to her on her desk and looked into her eyes.

He reached down, this time with a different tentacle, as the other one still encircled her wrist. From his position, he could not see the screen or the keyboard and was – in effect – entering data from a blind, upside down and backward position.

'Space, space, space. ICH'.

She debated whether to allow this impossible dialogue to continue or to run out screaming for someone from her crew to immediately re-certify her sanity.

She entered…

'Space, space, space. ICH+8 :)'

EIGHT responded now with a third tentacle.

'Space, space, space. 8+ICH :)'

Ichica could not deny that she was witnessing a special cephalopod indeed.

The research was soon completed on the edge of the Gyre. The Nisshin Maru sailed full speed ahead to the port of Long Beach to rendezvous with the new team of Californian statisticians. Ichica still had work to do, but the phenomenal performance of this rogue octopus was such a hit with the crew that she was given *carte blanche* to work exclusively with EIGHT. His learning curve was precipitous. EIGHT added five words each day to his vocabulary, a rate which soon doubled and doubled again. The goal of turning EIGHT into a circus performer was rejected and upgraded when it became clear the invertebrate surpassed everyone's expectations. Pretending to predict the winner of the next World Cup would be an insult to EIGHT's intelligence.

Once the Californians managed to overcome the notion that EIGHT and his "act" was not an elaborate prank, two developments came in rapid succession.

First, EIGHT was given a voice – literally, a voice. From now on, EIGHT's typed words – all in his presumed second language of Japanese- would be read and amplified into a digitally produced human voice. EIGHT now had at his disposal male or female voices, English with American or British accent, French, Japanese, Mandarin, and German. With a click on a drop-down bar of options – EIGHT could speak as clear as a native. He typed sixty words per minute. By bringing additional appendages to the task, he increased his performance to 150 wpm by week's end. An average person speaks between 100 to 130 words per minute. 150 words per minute was the speed at which a professional voice-over artist might speak.

The second development was the formation of a plan to get EIGHT on the talk show circuit in LA. EIGHT could highlight the research done by the Nisshin Maru group, share facts about the effects of marine pollution, and become a spokesperson to discourage humanity from dumping in the oceans. That was assuming that EIGHT would cooperate.

As always in Los Angeles, someone on the crew knew someone who knew someone who could get EIGHT and Ichica booked on a talk show. They would start small and work up to the big time late-night programs.

EIGHT seemed willing to would cooperate only with Ichica. She worried. How would EIGHT respond to gabby talk show hosts, strange surroundings, commercial breaks, and bright lights? How would he travel by means other than jet propulsion through saltwater or riding suction-cupped tentacles across a slippery deck floor?

Ichica prepared EIGHT with simple messages about ocean pollution and humanity's role in the tragedy of our oceans. She was breaking new ground, but it became apparent that EIGHT could absorb information in a variety of ways, including watching videos and reading articles off the internet.

There seemed no limit to EIGHT's capacity to learn. He began reading on his own. What he might say when the cameras were rolling was anyone's guess. Ichica held practice sessions in the ship's cafeteria with a half dozen team members. They experimented with languages and voices and decided that EIGHT would have the vocalization of an English speaking male with a British accent. That seemed to give him added credibility and a bit of flair. On land, EIGHT was a well-kept secret, but by the date of the first on-air interview, a frenzy of reporters buzzed in front of the TV studio as EIGHT's van arrived.

Pat Harvey of CBS News was the anchor chosen to conduct the first interview. She was given little advance information. Ichica would accompany the interview, insisting her desk be brought in, that EIGHT's pan of water would be set in its usual place, and that her computer would serve as the interface for EIGHT to interact with Ms. Harvey.

A blanket covered EIGHT's aquarium as team members wheeled it from the van to the studio. EIGHT arrived as cool as ever; Ichica was nervous and sweaty. The team stood nervously by.

Ichica stumbled through her introduction and made a poor effort to explain the project, while EIGHT sat in his puddle of water and toyed with his beak.

After a painful silence, Pat asked Ichica for the name of the octopus. Suddenly EIGHT came alert and began typing, his writing instantly translated to electronic speech.

"888888888888888888. My name is 8. I'm an octopus. What is your name?"

"My name is Pat Harvey," she replied, flabbergasted, but then in an aside to Ichica, she said, "Is he talking? Or is that you? Did you program him to do th-?"

"I am talking," said EIGHT. "Pat, have you ever swum in the Great Pacific Gyre? It's like swimming in a sewer of plastic. Everything smells like shit. Petroleum, more accurately. Stinks and feels awful. Try it sometime. I did. Nearly killed me, but that might have been the OxyContin I was taking at the time."

Pat Henry looked at Ichica dumbfounded. "Is this a joke?"

Ichica tried to stammer out an explanation. EIGHT's tentacles typed in a flurry of movement.

"Ms. Henry, how does it feel to be a member of a species too dumb to save itself? If you had a few more arms and legs at your disposal, I can only guess you would strangle yourself. I suggest you read up on what is happening in the world, and if you can't stop this parade of death that accompanies humanity wherever it goes, you might apologize to me and creatures like me that are being exterminated every day by human stupidity. Only then should you feel free to kill yourself."

Pat Henry would not stand for insults. She assumed she was being punked, and cut to a commercial. She refused to speak further to the research team and walked out. The producer ran a pre-recorded piece about a gay quilting group in town for the weekend Country Arts Festival.

Ichica and her colleagues had not witnessed this side of EIGHT's character. The appearance was a disaster, but it was a miracle in the same breath, and if the Nisshin Maru crew could find a way to harness EIGHT's ability and attitude, this was a pot of gold dropped into their laps.

The second taping went long and large. Graham Norton heard about EIGHT's appearance on the CBS local station in Los Angeles and decided this was too good to pass up. He was vacationing the US and could come wherever convenient for an interview. He had doubts about the legitimacy of EIGHT, especially EIGHT's mastery of human language, but even if it was phony, it had the potential for comedic theatre. He booked an interview.

Norton was great with EIGHT and left certain there was at least some legitimacy to EIGHT's "act" as he called it. EIGHT was splendid.

"So do you eat chicken?" asked Graham out of the blue?

"Who doesn't?" asked EIGHT. "Unlucky bird. They say it tastes like Octopus, but I can't imagine."

"And – pardon me for the indelicacy – how do Octopi ... procreate?" asked Graham.

"First, it's Octopuses, not Octopi. Your rules, not mine. Octopuses are quite sexy if you can get past the cannibalism. Or the very unsexy pollution. Or the spear of an angler who might snatch your mate from your arms. I'm no expert. Frankly, no octopus is, since we all pretty much die after our first fuck."

"You're still a virgin?" Asked Graham.

"Not exactly," answered EIGHT. My mate was killed in the heat of coitus. But had we consummated the deed, I'd be dead now instead of talking to you on TV."

"Wow, rough life!"

"Yeah, safer to masturbate." (Pause). "I'm kidding!"

"Is there a dating app for octopi? I mean octopuses?" asked Graham.

"Yeah, nobody swipes right faster than me!"

It was – by comparison – a success, but Ichica was not pleased.

"You didn't speak about pollution! Or the environment. You didn't say anything about our work on the Nisshin Maru."

"People don't want to hear it!" said EIGHT. "They prefer sex jokes and movie star gossip. I don't understand how you live as you do."

Ichica was hurt. She was being lumped into a group of all humans, the human gene pool, who normally didn't think twice about dumping garbage into the oceans and discarding toxic chemicals in the air. Ichica was innocent of those crimes.

"We're not all bad, EIGHT!" said Ichica. But she knew as she said it that bad humans outnumbered good humans by a factor of twenty to one.

Conan hosted the next live interview, humorous but credible, and EIGHT was able to explain how the smell and the film of petroleum permeate everything handled by humans. Smell, feel, and taste. Though humans weren't equipped to sense it, it was present in everything humans touched.

EIGHT disrupted the show by flirting with and later making a clumsy attempt at fingering a guest actor, who screamed as she rushed back to the Green Room. It took her several minutes to quiet down and Conan asked EIGHT to leave.

Steven Colbert hosted a guest appearance, and EIGHT entered juggling, wearing a hat and a scarf. With some prompting from Steven, EIGHT discussed 'the sixth extinction,' the extermination event experienced five times in the history of the planet.

It was the saddest and most powerful appearance to date. Colbert was gobsmacked.

In his appearance on 'Fox and Friends,' EIGHT ridiculed and humiliated the trio of presenters. EIGHT followed their guest Scott Pruitt – ex-EPA director. While making small talk with the three co-hosts, EIGHT slipped his tentacles behind the sofa where Pruitt was seated and wrapped one about Pruitt's neck. As Pruitt gagged, EIGHT and Ichica escaped in the confusion.

EIGHT's last appearance was on Letterman when EIGHT predicted his own death. "I know you all wish to eat me. Or kill me. You are all murderers. One day it will happen. You humans think you are god-like, but in fact, you are the devil. You feel the need to take us all with you to hell."

Ichica was overwhelmed by the impact EIGHT was having, but sad that it was more a circus than a promotion of her scientific research and findings. EIGHT was proving to be incorrigible and completely free-spirited. Requests for bookings flowed in, but EIGHT seemed uninterested in talking further or planning appearances with Ichica. Ichica grew worried when he stopped eating and refused her attention. She sadly went to bed, feeling like she had lost a friend.

The next day, EIGHT slipped over the side of the Nisshin Maru and into the bay. He left a message for Ichica.

"Clean up the filth. Hurry. 8."

HOW WAS YOUR DAY?

So I figured something out. If you enjoy having dreams at night, eat a big meal just before you sleep. The bigger the meal, the later you consume it, the sooner thereafter you crawl into bed, the bigger and more outrageous will be your dream. I am not necessarily recommending this course of action; I am simply putting into words a cause and effect relationship which may or may not be of interest or of service to you.

Remembering your dream is another matter. A dream is like a slick quick trout momentarily within your grasp, such that you must act swiftly and decisively to capture it. Otherwise, it goes abruptly over the side and disappears beneath the murky waters of memory, never to be seen again. To my current way of thinking, that is where most dreams – and most trout - belong.

However, last night's dream was …. Well, I would like to say an exception, but by the end of this tale, I am hoping you can tell me.

So let's start with the dream. I (all dreams begin with "I.") am sitting there at the edge of a forest, minding my business, when a small Native American girl appears before me, dressed in deer hide, holding a hand-carved hickory bow, and carrying three river cane arrows nested in a quiver of white oak splits. It is early evening and a hunter moon is low and bright. The girl is walking on a narrow trail. She is not childlike and playful, but rather serious and determined. I follow her.

She approaches a tree, a soft maple, brightly colored red and orange in leaves soon to fall. From a medium distance, she raises her bow, notches an arrow, pulls back, aims, and fires. She hits the tree dead center.

The tree begins to gush black fluid from the wound made by the girl's arrow. It withers and dies before my eyes, and becomes nothing more than a pool of viscous liquid on the sandy trail. The girl retrieves the arrow from the pool, wipes it off on a selected leaf, and returns it to the quiver on her back. She trots away into darkness.

Switch to me again, now seated at an office desk, talking on a phone. I hear nothing of the conversation but know its content. I am invited by a famous film director to play a part in the recreation of a scene from a dream he has had. As he explains the dream, I realize it is the same dream I have just recounted. How can I say no? I agree to appear in his film, but the dream ends before I can meet my young co-star, before I can become rich and famous.

I am now in the Western Smokey Mountains with my wife to see the fall colors. I have been worried we would miss the autumn spectacle, but as it turns out we have arrived just in time. Our goal for the day is to visit Yellow Creek Falls. It is a short hike, shorter and easier than either of the two falls we had hiked to the day before. Still, I manage to fall into the swift-moving stream and soak my clothes and shoes in the cold water. I'm never in danger, except for the possible danger of catching a cold, but I'm certainly exposed to humiliation. We could have dashed for home, but I had promised lunch to my wife and she doesn't do well when she is hungry. I decide I can survive the temporary hardship of wet jeans and shirt and squishy tennis shoes. My phone miraculously survives.

The restrooms at our chosen restaurant on the Little Tennessee River have washers and dryers right inside, so I strip naked and toss shirt, socks, jeans, and underwear into the dryer, put the dial on high heat, and dash to an empty stall as my wife waits for a table in the restaurant. After ten minutes, I get her text saying that she has been seated, so I wait a few minutes more for the restroom to clear, then dash for the dryer, seize my clothes now nearly dry, dress, and join my wife looking almost normal.

We are at a place famous for its curvy roads, especially a section of Route 129 called "Tail of the Dragon," which features 318 curves in just under 11 miles. What can make many people very sick seems to make bikers and sports car drivers very happy. At the restaurant, we see huge bikes, huge bikers, huge biker's huge girlfriends, and slightly smaller sports car drivers in abundance. I am intrigued by how friendly and nice they all are, especially the Bikers and Biker Babes. They seem to love taking selfies of each other in their biker gear. The sports car people blend in a bit better with the normal-sized civilians but appear to be nice too as they explore the fall colors just like us.

On our way home, we follow behind a slow-moving truck on a narrow and curvy road. The truck is mounted with a heavy crane, and an ungainly counterweight protrudes out in front like a battering ram. As we descend a steep grade on Route 143 approaching a T-intersection with Route 28, the truck backfires loudly in protest. Total brake failure follows, leading to a sudden shocking accident. Just out of view around the bend, the truck flips onto its side, spilling oil and diesel on the road, blocking traffic from three directions. In seconds, a quiet spot in the country transforms into a place of danger, excitement, and emergency.

My wife normally loses her cool in emergencies, but for some reason today she steps from the car like a superhero and immediately begins directing traffic and working her way to the epicenter of the action. I try to help with the traffic by signaling a car to come forward when the fellow further up the highway has just done the same to a car coming from the opposite direction. This ends in a Mexican standoff, and I decide I am perhaps better suited for some other task. I take my leave and would have been happy to go back to sit in my car and sulk, but the owner of one of the vehicles first on the scene and parked haphazardly in the middle of the highway shouts at me to please move his truck out of the way.

This I do. It is some kind of a power company service vehicle, obviously the man's place of business, full of tools and wire and spare parts and soda cans and cigarette butts, such that little room is afforded to a driver. I squeeze in, find reverse, park further back up the highway and off the pavement, and return the keys to the driver who is still midway in the road directing traffic in graceful coordination with wife, who stands further down the road. Although 50 yards apart, it's like a scene from Dirty Dancing how they work so well together without ever having met.

Emergency vehicles and technicians show up, so my wife and I squeeze through the line of cars and return home. I need a shower as my wet clothes are still wet after all. I take a hot shower and fall into bed, exhausted despite it being only 4 in the afternoon. I am awakened by my wife who says that I HAVE TO SEE the sunset, so I drag myself to the front porch and witness a truly spectacular scene of red, white, and blue stripes above the Smokey Mountain National Forrest.

My friend Jim, an ex-rock and roll singer and a tug boat captain drives up and invites us to our neighbor Buddy's house to watch the baseball game. Jim is with his son Rod. They recently found each other. It turns out Jim had a passionate one-nighter with Rod's mother some forty years ago but had no idea a child was produced until a long string of coincidences including a message in a bottle brought them together. Rod comes complete with wife and two kids, now Jim's instant family. They couldn't be happier to be together.

So it turns out Buddy isn't home but that doesn't seem to matter so we watch the game there after all. Buddy has a date planned with Veronica, the event planner from Tapoco Lodge where I used the clothes dryer, but Buddy gets turned back by the truck accident on the highway - still obstructing traffic hours later - and returns to find his house full of people watching the baseball game. He doesn't mind at all and lights a fire in the fireplace, serves us all soup, and we watch the Yankees salvage their chances by staving off elimination by the Astros.

I awaken each morning now and for the past three years feeling four or five bricks hit me on the head, and I think the sky is falling. I tell people "The sky is falling!" but some 35 to 40% of the people I tell don't believe me, and get angry at me for saying so. And I got kicked out of my book club last month for swearing. I said, "What the fuck, Maria?"

So, now, you tell me. Please! How does one know when he or she is dreaming?

END OF VIOLENCE

Elwin had seen much violence in life. He hunted pheasant and deer with his father. He boxed in high school and won trophies. In junior college, he suffered the humiliation of losing a bar fight and swore he'd never lose another. His date chose to accept his invitation to make her real boyfriend jealous. At the Busy Bee Tavern, her true love came in on cue as Elwin ordered a second round. The football tackle approached from behind and cold-cocked him. Witnesses said that Tiffany smiled through the brief struggle and left cuddling the beefy arm of her real boyfriend, not bothering to say goodbye, thanks for dinner, or are you alright?

Once his broken jaw healed, Elwin joined a Mixed Martial Arts Club, and learned not only how to fight but also how to hurt. He began cage fighting and never lost a match. He curtailed his fighting career by enlisting in the Marines, together with his friend and classmate Sean.

Before leaving for Afghanistan, he married his school sweetheart Sybil. She sat ringside at his matches and screamed encouragement, from the first whistle until the winner was declared. It was not a marriage made in heaven. From his base in Kabul, Elwin grew suspicious when her letters suddenly stopped and his calls went unanswered.

His assignment terminated early when he was stabbed in the neck by a teenage girl on the street. He was awarded a purple heart. His friend Sean re-upped for a second tour but came home in worse condition. His legs were blown off by an IED. Doctors patched him up but couldn't fix his mind. He was alcoholic, paraplegic, and mean.

As suspected, Elwin's wife abandoned him for a man who he would have fought if he'd not chosen to enlist. She gave birth to a daughter while Elwin was away. Yes, she was Elwin's, but she barely knew him. After the breakup, Sybil went off with her lover, and Elwin - too diminished to raise a daughter - begged his mother-in-law for help and sent Sofia to live with her. The temporary arrangement became permanent.

His own mother was not an option: she died in a car wreck two years earlier.

For eleven years he squandered his GI benefits, collected unemployment, and sold weed. Everyone did it. A deal soured when a buyer pulled a gun instead of a wallet from his jacket. Elwin was quick, kicking him hard enough to break his pelvis and several bones in his face. For this, he served a year in a low-security penitentiary, a shorter sentence than it might have been thanks to his honorable discharge from the service. When he walked out of jail, he decided he was done with violence. He wasn't sure how, but he committed to living in peace. He was thirty-two. His daughter Sofia was thirteen.

Four elements converged at once. Had any one of them not occurred when it did, Elwin's plan would never have been conceived. But they did, and his path became clear. Whether a good or a bad choice, his course was set.

First was his wish to make a clean break from his current life. Second was his mother-in-law's decision to marry a man Elwin knew to be a scoundrel, certifying that his daughter would not be safe living with her any longer. Third, his damaged Marine friend was facing drug charges and threatening suicide. And finally, his rich Uncle Henry from Argentina invited him to move in with him on his peanut farm. Elwin decided to make the leap, move to Cordoba, and take his daughter and friend with him.

His friend Sean was on board but penniless. He was confined to a wheelchair, chain-smoked unfiltered Camels, and had failing health. He was barely presentable to the public. Daughter Sofia barely knew Elwin, despised the idea of moving to a foreign country and swore to resist him every step of the way. None of them spoke Spanish. None had traveled abroad except to go to war.

Elwin managed to appease Sofia temporarily by promising to buy her a horse of her own. He had several conversations by phone with his uncle, and it seemed he and his entourage would be welcomed. Elwin got few specifics from Uncle Henry, but the old man kept insisting there was '*no problema*.' He offered to buy three business class tickets on *Aerolineas Argentinas* three weeks hence. Elwin hadn't felt this excited since he first deployed to Afghanistan. That hadn't turned out so well. This time he hoped for better. All three travelers needed a serious and immediate change of scene.

Sofia packed a week early which Elwin considered a good sign. Sean, his paraplegic buddy, packed a duffel that could not have held more than a few changes of genes and t-shirts and maybe a toiletry bag though he didn't shave and sometimes gave the impression he didn't bathe either. Elwin worried about what to bring but for the life of him couldn't think of anything but the absolute basics. Uncle Henry instructed him to bring birth certificates and health information but didn't say why, only that he would be taking care of everything. Elwin felt ill-equipped to think for anyone beyond himself, but he swore to try his best to help both Sean and Sofia land softly and find their way.

They'd be a family, he hoped. It was possible, but he admitted it was risky.

They arrived in Buenos Aires, and faced navigating the huge international airport to make their connections, first to a smaller domestic airport an hour across town, and then on to their connecting flight to Cordoba City, where Uncle Henry promised he would be waiting for them.

He wasn't. Instead, a hired hand appeared, holding a sign with Elwin's name. He loaded the three and their skimpy bags into a Hilux pickup and drove too fast from the city of Cordoba to the small town called Hernandez, the Peanut Capital of Argentina. When Elwin heard about Henry's farm, he had imagined something more akin to a ranch in Colorado or Wyoming, with cattle and grain and horses and ... well, not a peanut farm. But what the hell. He liked peanut butter.

The hired hand was named Adrian, and he worked with Uncle Henry for years. He said Henry wasn't feeling well enough for the trip, which is why Adrian came instead.

"Is he sick?" asked Elwin.

"He's very sick," said Adrian. "Do you know about Henry's illness?"

"No. I didn't know he was sick. Is it serious?" asked Elwin.

"I'm surprised he didn't mention it," said Adrian. "Listen, you had better talk to him." He said no more about it, and they rode silently to their prospective new home.

The place was everything they hoped for but nothing they

expected as if on the checklist of all good things there was an asterisk after each item. There was a big house, beautiful but run down. There was a pool. It was covered in green algae. There were horses which you couldn't get near, as no one had ridden them in years. There was a big TV; no cable or antennae. There was a yard with knee-high grass. There were fruit trees, with most of the crop rotting on the ground. There was a fireplace with a collapsed chimney, making it dangerous to use until repaired.

The countryside was expansive. The little town of Hernandez twenty minutes away appeared to be straight out of the 1950s.

Elwin would take Sofia to ask about schools. There was little information available. Elwin had promised Sofia if she didn't like the school he would home-school her. Neither one was sure which of the two options frightened them most. Sofia had grown quiet since they arrived.

Sean had hurdles too. The sidewalks were broken and uneven, so his mobility was compromised. Uncle Henry had promised to build a ramp up to the front door, but his ramp consisted of two loose planks with no supports, and if Sean tried to make it up unassisted, he'd end up on his head. Uncle Henry –they were told – was visiting his doctor in town. So much for the warm welcome.

"Is there any food, Adrian?" Elwin asked. "Sofia and Sean are hungry."

Elwin too was famished but was already feeling guilty that he had just made a huge mistake and all three of them would be paying for it for years to come. They could turn around and head back and try Plan B, except they didn't have a Plan B, and they didn't have more than a few hundred bucks between them.

Adrian said there were cold cuts in the fridge. He put them out with some fresh bread, and though it was a primitive way to eat, it was delicious.

"Any beer?" asked Sean. Sure enough, Adrian found a few, a local brand that wasn't bad. He offered Sofia a coke but she said she hated coke. He said the well water was both good and safe to drink and this Sofia confirmed, not by saying so but by drinking three glasses back-to-back. Elwin observed it was funny how you don't think much about good water unless there is none. Lots of things went like that, he guessed.

Uncle Henry came home driving a pick-up, and Adrian went out to help him come in. Elwin was disturbed to see how weak he looked and overheard Adrian chewing him out for driving on his own. They spoke in Spanish and Elwin could only guess what was said, but it seemed clear that Uncle Henry was a stubborn old coot, and that Adrian was at the limits of his patience.

"Hello, Elwin!" he said as he approached the porch, Sean in his wheelchair, Elwin on a three-legged stool, and Sofia nestled in a porch swing that squeaked like it was ready to fall.

"Give me a hug there, young fellow. Last time we met you were half your size. You grew up! And who's this here?" he said as he looked to Sofia.

"Hello," said Sofia, none too friendly. She was agitated about everything but polite enough to say hello. She had her faults but shyness wasn't one of them.

Elwin had to direct Uncle Henry's attention to Sean, as he did what so many do, ignored a handicap to avoid any discomfort from looking at it. And Sean was not easy to look at. He wore a grizzly beard and smelled ripe. Henry started in his direction, perhaps to shake his hand, but thought better of it, and decided to conserve his few remaining watts of energy by leaning against the doorway.

"Tell you what," he said, "Let's have a nice dinner tonight and open a few bottles of wine while we sit around and get to know each other. I for one am dead on my feet and if I don't go lay down, I may fall down if you get my drift. Say about 8 o'clock here on the veranda for drinks? I have my English-speaking cook and ex-girlfriend coming over to prepare the meal, and you can all have a lay down too if you like." He started moving to the door. "Nothing I hate worse than getting on an airplane except maybe getting off an airplane. It's like finally getting comfortable in your coffin and then having to get up and leave it." His voice faded as he disappeared inside the house.

Both Sean and Sofia turned to Elwin with looks that said, "WTF did you get us into?"

As he lay resting in his room, Elwin replayed the conversation, picking over it for details he might have missed the first time around. Uncle Henry used the words 'dead,' 'fall down,' and 'coffin' all in one short burst. Henry hired a cook to make dinner, either for tonight's meal or perhaps as a normal arrangement. Cooks make life easier, that was for sure. Elwin knew he didn't feel like preparing a meal that night. And Henry didn't say 'open a bottle,' he said 'open some bottles.' Elwin heard about Argentine wine and it sounded good, but Henry in his condition shouldn't be drinking alcohol, and Sean could get crazy fast when the booze was flowing. Elwin hoped Sofia hadn't started drinking yet, but who knew? She was an adolescent and there were worse things she could be doing. If they had stayed at home, Sofia would be drinking plus having sex and maybe doing drugs. Not because of a flawed character, just because that was what kids did.

Had Elwin known it would be one of his last conversations with Uncle Henry, he would have gone into it prepared with a tight agenda, a list of questions, and a note pad. Instead, the four of them felt each other out, each one with the other participants at the table. The meal was lovely, the wine lovelier still. Uncle Henry was charming as Elwin had remembered the one time they had met 20 years back and spent a few days together with his mother- Henry's sister- and Elwin's dad. Elwin didn't know then that his mom and dad were divorcing, and that Uncle Henry was there specifically to make sure Elwin's mother didn't get mistreated. They had gone to a small resort and played euchre and sang songs to Henry's accompaniment on the guitar. Elwin's father was distant, his mother was broken-hearted, and Henry kept everyone civil. They tried to figure out how the family would move forward. Elwin was Sophia's age at the time and thought he knew everything but in fact, he knew nothing.

Regrettably Uncle Henry – like most humans – felt like his life would never end, so he felt no pressure to make clear his plans for Elwin and Sofia, his plans for the farm, and the incalculable number of details which could have made a difference if only Elwin knew. Instead, the vast array of problems were dropped into his lap like screaming babies and frying pans aflame.

Again, he replayed the conversation over in his mind as he was prone to do, to search for tidbits of intelligence that he had missed the first time, assuming like Uncle Henry that he had all the time in the world to figure things out. This was necessary because Uncle Henry never woke up, not that morning, and not any morning thereafter. The doctor said he suffered an aneurysm and heart attack that took him without the slightest notion that he would never be coming back.

What Elwin recalled from the dinner conversation of the night before was the following:

The horses were nags but could be replaced in a heartbeat by putting out the word they were interested in new mounts. A neighbor raised thoroughbreds for a breeder who raced them in Mar del Plata and La Plata, and if a horse didn't win a race by the time it turned three, he gave it away. It cost too much to keep a racehorse that generated no income. They were marvelous beasts but could run right out from under you before you knew they were prepped to go.

Henry told them that the cook was undependable except in the bedroom and in her table fare and that Adrian- while disloyal - was a great assistant if there was nothing on the table to steal.

They learned that Uncle Henry had lots of money but what he did not have was energy or time.

They learned that this beautiful and productive farm would kill you if you didn't pay attention. And they learned that the whole town was angry with him, owed him money, or was jealous. They were interested only in his land, his money, and his *laissez-faire* attitude.

Uncle Henry said he planned to go over some papers with Elwin on the following day, but Elwin knew nothing of what those papers concerned, or where they were tucked away. Nor did he know that Uncle Henry's land was worth about 14 million dollars.

Uncle Henry lay dead in his bed the next morning and Elwin was there with his young daughter and his damaged friend without knowing Uncle Henry's grand vision and with no vision of his own.

His first interaction with Adrian put Elwin on the defensive, as Adrian seemed all too eager to see the group capitulate and depart. Elwin had been contemplating doing that very thing, but he was in no mood to be pushed. He told Adrian he planned to stay awhile, and that he should not mention their departure again unless Elwin brought it up. Adrian's reaction was enough to convince him that he had a vested interest in keeping their visit short.

Adrian stayed in a small guest house some meters from the main house, and once Uncle Henry was in the ground, Elwin saw Adrian approaching the main house with several boxes and suitcases. It appeared he planned to move into Uncle Henry's room. This was not going to happen as long as Elwin was around. He spoke to the cook and asked her what she thought. While she might not be trustworthy, she had no love for Adrian and said he should tell Adrian to go fuck himself. This Elwin did in only slightly less colorful language. And the cook said another important thing. She suggested that Elwin immediately visit Uncle Henry's *escribano* in town. According to the cook, the *escribano* would know what Uncle Henry had in mind for the future. At that point, Elwin had no idea what an *escribano* was, a cross between a lawyer and a notary.

Escribano Jorge Montero offered Elwin a chair and even a

cafecito in his living room/office on a side street in Hernandez. They sat in silence facing each other across a rustic wooden table. It was about as uncomfortable as one could get, neither speaking to the other. It reminded Elwin of his divorce negotiations with his ex-wife Sibyl when their two lawyers left the room to talk. He sat across from her passing hateful glances between them. He thought for a moment about his new family.

Sofia and Sean were exploring the farm. Sofia was interested in the barns, the horse tackle, and with luck, she might even lay eyes on the horses if they decided to wonder in close from their hangout in the far corner of the field most distant from human interference. One gelding in particular looked robust if not friendly. She planned to lay out a bit of grain to lure him to the barn. She might get a rope around his neck or a halter positioned over his unkempt forelock. That was the idea, at least.

Sean, it turned out, was a skilled mechanic before his military service, fixing wrecks and even racing stock-cars on occasion. He wanted to look over the tractor, wagon, planter, and harvester parked in the dusty shed. If he could get something running they might be able to sell it and apply the money for some other improvements or tickets home. Or buy some decent whiskey if it could be had anywhere. There was also an old hot tub next to the pool that caught his eye. His stubs still hurt, and his back was always out of whack from sitting on his ass all day in that 'wheely chair' as Sofia called it. The hot tub was filthy and the pump was busted like everything else. And there was no tavern nearby to spend his time and money, and though everything the paraplegic did was doubly difficult, he was not one to sit on his butt and do nothing.

After a long silence, the *escribano* waiting for Elwin to play his first card, and Elwin mustering the courage to speak in Spanish, they blurted out their opening statements at the same moment.

"*No hablo mucho espanol,*" said Elwin.

"I suppose you are here about the Will," said *Escribano* Jorge in perfect English.

Elwin won that round, revealing nothing but his ignorance of the language, while the *escribano* revealed his mastery of English, some knowledge about Elwin's situation, a hint at Henry's intentions, and the fact that a Will existed somewhere.

Like mountain goats, both backed up and faced off for a second charge.

"Yes, I want to discuss the Will," said Elwin.

"What do you wish to discuss?" asked the *escribano*.

"What's in it," said Elwin.

"What do you think is in it?" asked the *escribano*.

This was a tango in the most traditional style, two men as it used to be, dancing around a fine point, teasing and attacking as in a bout of fencing; lunge and parry, riposte, and counter. Where was this going and how would it end?

"Your Uncle came to me two months ago and made his wishes known," said Jorge. "My question to you is, what do you know and what do you intend to do with the farm?"

"Do with the farm?" thought Elwin. "As if it were mine to do something with it?"

"What were my uncle's wishes?"

"You must bring me the will signed by your Uncle. There are procedures to be followed."

"You must have a copy."

"Of course I have a copy."

"Please show it to me."

"Why must I show it? Have you never discussed this with your Uncle?"

"He died the morning after I arrived. Give me a break," Elwin ordered.

"What do you plan to do?"

"Why does that matter to you?"

"Will you join the consortium?"

"Why is that your concern?"

"I think we're done here."

"What?" Elwin asked incredulously.

"Bring me the Will and we'll talk," said the *escribano*.

"But…"

"Good day."

Elwin hired the cook to return and make dinner and said he wanted to secure her services, but until he settled and began to show income, it could be only one day per week.

"I will come three days a week," she said. "You pay me later."

"What do you know about Uncle Henry's will?" he asked her.

"Very little."

"Very little is more than me," Elwin said.

"He said he was planning to make one," she said.

"Did he?"

"I don't know," she said. "If he did it's in his room or the wall safe behind the picture."

"Show me."

"I don't have a key or combination."

"I'll break in if necessary."

They did. It was empty.

"Maybe Adrian knows something," Elwin suggested.

"If he does, he won't tell you," she revealed.

"That's a problem," Elwin admitted.

At dinner, he explained the situation to Sean and Sofia.

"Hell with that," said Sean. "Let's search his room."

"He is there now," said Sofia. "We have to get him out."

"I'll insist he give me a tour of the property tomorrow," said Elwin. "While we're gone, you two search his rooms."

They found the will. The cook translated it. It awarded the farm, the house, the money, and virtually everything to Elwin. It gave a painting to the cook and a statue to Adrian. Elwin fired Adrian the next day.

Taking over the farm was as hard as anything Elwin had ever done, but with Sean's help, he managed. Henry had fought with the local agricultural laborers union. They not only refused to work for him, but they threatened that if he didn't settle with the union and pay five years of retroactive fees, they would use any means necessary to disrupt the production on the land.

Henry had planted a peanut crop, but only in late May, putting the harvest at risk of frost in late November when the crop would be ready for picking. Sean worked brilliantly on the shed to make it 'legless friendly.' He rigged ladders up horizontally so that from his wheelchair he could lift himself and move above the machinery to fix and fine-tune, to paint and repair, until the tractor, the wagon, and the harvester were all in working order. If they couldn't get Union labor, they'd do it themselves.

Probate of the Will might take eighteen months to two years. There would be no money from the estate until then. The crop had to be harvested if they were to stay afloat. They sold the planter to pay for the gas needed to run the tractor and the harvester. If they managed a harvest, they would buy a new seeder next year in April. If they didn't get the harvest in, there would be no crop next year.

Sean modified the controls so that he could drive the harvester with no legs. Elwin ran the tractor, pulling the wagon, offloading the harvester, transporting to the dryer bins, auguring the grain off the back of the wagon and into the steel storage structures. Sofia rode *Damelo* to school during the day. She had given up on the farm nags and went straight to the source to request a non-winner three-year-old for free. She became their runner, delivering sandwiches, coffee, and messages to Sean and Elwin in the fields.

Then came the day when the stars aligned, relegating them to chaos. Sean was running the harvester, finishing the lower fields with only the back 100 hectares left to harvest. Elwin made seven trips with full loads of peanuts. The larger grain bin was full and a second smaller bin was half full. Elwin didn't like the look of the sky.

He saw Sofia riding towards him when the wind picked up suddenly and the temperature dropped. It was going to be a near thing. He could see Sean moving across the field, his back to the weather. Elwin hoped he had the sense to come in. Then the sky opened up, not with rain but with hail.

The hail appeared as tiny ice chips which stung but did no damage. The wind gusted and there was every indication it would worsen before it got better. A huge black mushroom cloud formed and began swirling around a point directly over Hernandez.

Sofia shouted that the syndicate rep came by and threatened to stop the harvest. There was a group of men and trucks gathering on the road in front of the entrance. She told them to fuck off and rode out with coffee and *jamon crudo y queso* sandwiches.

Elwin smiled when she told of her confrontation, and he urged her to ride hard to meet Sean and tell him to get to shelter because the hail was getting bigger and the wind stronger.

She took off, and what a thing of beauty it was. Her horse ran faster than any Elwin had seen outside a racetrack. The horse's tail and Sofia's ponytail streamed out behind. She leaned over the horse's neck and flew. She pulled alongside Sean's harvester at the moment the sky went dark and the hailstorm began in earnest. Elwin raced for the barn with a half-empty load, hoping to make it to shelter before he was forced to take refuge under the wagon. A gust suddenly hit him, lifting the rig up on two wheels. He adjusted direction to avoid another strike from the side. The wind pounded.

Elwin looked back but could see nothing of Sean or Sofia or the harvester. He made it to the barn and pulled inside. Hail the size of lemons was piling on the ground. He ran out to the truck and drove in behind the wagon. One window was already broken and the roof and hood were dented. Four inches of hail piled in the truck bed.

Still no sign of Sofia. No horse. No harvester. Ice balls the size of grapefruit were smashing at the door. There were places where ice was stacked a foot deep. Elwin sat in the truck, ready to sacrifice it to the gods when the air grew suddenly still. The hail stopped. He drove out cautiously and looked to the skies for funnel clouds. There were none. He drove the slippery dirt road towards where he had last seen the harvester. His stomach leaped when he saw the harvester on its side. Then he made out an almost unidentifiable blob of life two-hundred meters towards home. Drawing close he identified the form of the horse on the ground. Sofia was lying across its head and neck, and Sean's shortened form lay across Sofia's upper body. Elwin ran to them and began coaxing them up. First Sean. Then Sofia. Then the horse *Damelo*.

Sofia had managed to extract Sean from the cab of the capsized harvester and with what must have been superhuman strength, hoisted him up behind her. They began their way back, pummeled by the hail, Sean doing his best to cover Sofia. A huge ball of ice hit the horse in the nose and brought it to its knees. Sofia dismounted and laid across the horse's head. Sean crawled to Sofia and covered her with his own body. The three were battered unmercifully, covered in bruises. But none – including the horse – suffered a mortal wound. When ready, *Damelo* rocked onto his stomach, rose up on wobbly legs, and shuddered. They hugged and made their way back to the house.

The syndicate workers had fled, and Elwin drove to the tiny hospital in Hernandez where both Sofia and Sean were examined and released. The horse was head cut but fine. The harvester was damaged but insured, and Sean said he could fix it anyway.

In the hot tub that night the three of them recovered, comparing bruises and discussing impressions of the day's events.

Within a year, Sean found work as a handyman and started a relationship with the cook. Sofia finished high school and learned jumping and dressage. Elwin opened a boxing school in Hernandez. Life settled into a routine. Both farm and family flourished.

And Elwin remembered. He came with his family to escape violence. He learned that violence will find you. Violence knows where you live.

ACKNOWLEDGMENTS

THANK YOU

...to George Oswald, the English Department at Illinois State University, William Wantling, Margaret Thompson, good teachers all. And to my English Speaking Writers Group in Buenos Aires.

WORDS ARE LIKE NETS
THAT ENSNARE THE FLOW OF LIFE.

ABOUT THE AUTHOR

Cliff Williamson is a school teacher, business owner, bartender, musician, world traveler, and father of two. He and his wife Marcia divide their time between homes in Buenos Aires, Sarasota, and the Smokey Mountains. Cliff is a writer of poetry, short stories, and articles on business excellence. He has written the novel, Shining New Testament.

facebook.com/Cliff-Williamson-101585178393096
instagram.com/cliffallenwilliamson

Made in the USA
Coppell, TX
04 February 2023